A Sham Betrothal

❧ *Georgians in Paris* ❧

Jennie Goutet

Copyright © 2024 by Jennie Goutet

All rights reserved.

No part of this book may be reproduced in any form or by any electronic or mechanical means, including information storage and retrieval systems, without written permission from the author, except for the use of brief quotations in a book review.

Development edit by Jolene Perry @ Waypoint Authors

Proof edit by Theresa Schultz @ Marginalia Editing

Cover Design by Shaela Odd @ Blue Water Books

To Peace Williams, who shares a birthday of sorts with this book.

CHAPTER 1

July 1774
Paris, France

"*Morbleu*, but it's hot."

Basile Gervain, reluctant marquis of Verdelle, stood on rue Montorgeuil in Les Halles in front of the *pâtisserie* Stohrer, whose wafts of emanating heat carried out the scent of fresh pastries. He was dressed elaborately—unlike the raiment he wore on his own estate—his light gray waistcoat embroidered with a black floral pattern peeping out from his dark gray silk coat. His unpowdered hair was tied in a queue under a black cocked hat, trimmed with a somber silk ribbon, and below his slim breeches, clocked stockings disappeared into buckled shoes with the scantest heel as was the fashion of the day.

To his left, his friend Grégoire St. Pierre stood beside a shop with a clanging bell on the vitrified door that sold jewelry to the bourgeois and more modest of the noble class. He was equally distinguished in appearance though more restrained in temperament. A man of few words, Grégoire dressed in as sober a fashion as his long-suffering valet would allow him, a muted style which suited his tall, lanky form.

"'Tis true, *en effet*." Greg removed his hat and with it gently stirred the air next to his face before replacing it on his head.

They were waiting for their companion, the *Vicomte* de Galladier, to purchase a token piece of jewelry, for he had fallen in love yet again, to their infinite amusement. Armand de Galladier was born with the soul of a poet and could not resist the call of a blushing face. Unfortunately, he was not gifted with address and had not the success one would expect of a titled man of comfortable means. No one could call him above ordinary in terms of looks, with a weak chin and eyes that had a tendency to bulge. His declarations of love had always carried a tinge of desperation that rather sparked flight in the females he set his eye upon than compelled them to turn a demure face his way.

As they were all three of them young in years, having only just entered their third decade, Basile had no doubt his friend would settle on a woman who was pleased to return his regard before they were in their dotage. For the moment, however, they were pleased to encourage his efforts with teasing and ribaldry.

Opposite to where they waited was a *poissonnerie*, and the strong smell of fish reached them and mingled with the more pleasant scent of the sweet wine-infused *baba*, the specialty of this particular pastry shop. If there was any mercy to be had on this hot day, it was that no rain had appeared in a fortnight, and the refuse and horse droppings on the street contributed only minimally to the mingled perfumes of Paris. Another reason Basile preferred his home in Champagne. His chef produced fine meals and pastries only slightly inferior to Stohrer, and the scents there were of wheat and grass and flowers. It smelled *clean.*

A couple passed in front of them whom Basile suspected were English. The gentleman had a profusion of lace pouring from his sleeves with heeled shoes that were more ornamented than was fashionable. The lady wore a spring green *robe à l'anglaise* with an open skirt to reveal an underskirt embroidered in pink and silver silk threads. Her brown hair was lightly powdered in a similar tone and matched the color of her large eyes to perfection.

In general, Basile chose to allow the female sex to pass by unobserved. He had nearly become entrapped once, and the passage of time had only shown him how lucky was his escape. He much preferred sport and whatever games he might get up with his friends. But something about this English lady caught his attention, likely in the disparity between her queenly air and intelligent eyes and the stolid bulk and dull expression of her escort. Although she barely glanced at Basile, he had time to appreciate the sweet set of her lips, her aquiline nose, and those soft brown eyes.

As the couple entered Stohrer on his right, he swiveled to its entrance, wishing to confirm his hunch that they were indeed of the English race. Perhaps he and his friends might stop for a cup of coffee and a *viennoiserie* of some sort. It had been hours since they'd broken their fast, had it not? As he contemplated proposing it to his friend, a finicky English male voice reached him on the street through the open door of the bakery.

"I will have three of those pastries with the cream. You may wrap them for us. We will not be dining here."

A beat of silence fell, and then: *"Je suis désolée monsieur, mais je ne comprends rien à ce que vous dites."*

The corner of Basile's lips turned up. Stohrer was famous enough to have an English clientele, and the tradeswoman behind the counter likely spoke a little of the language. However, there had been no courtesy of a "good day," and unlike the Englishmen enlightened enough to speak French in a country of French-speakers, this one made no such attempt.

"I said," came the voice, a notch louder and more shrill, "three, THREE of those. The CREAM."

"Perhaps..." a gentle, womanly voice hinted.

"No, Sophie. It's intolerable that they should not speak God's own language. It's those cakes I am asking for. Those ones RIGHT THERE."

Basile listened to the tradeswoman repeat her avowal that she understood nothing, and he shook his head, his grin growing broader as the man repeated his request for the fourth time in a voice that ill hid his frustration. Basile peered into the shop where he spied the Englishman, red around the gills. To his right, the few patrons at the tables leaned in with whispers and muffled laughter.

The pretty Englishwoman stepped forward at last, and Basile managed to catch the low timbre of her words spoken firmly in nearly perfect French.

"*Bonjour*. Have the goodness to excuse the monsieur. It is not his fault if he is stupid. He would be pleased to take three of your *babas* if you would be so kind as to wrap them for us."

She stepped back, and the tradeswoman smiled at her and nodded as she set the requested pastries in paper and wrapped them with twine. "*Cela fera vingt et un sous.*"

"The price is twenty-one sous," the Englishwoman

repeated to her compatriot. Basile watched as her mask of English indifference shrouded the interesting show of character he had just been witness to when she spoke French.

She couldn't be the man's wife, or that was the greatest piece of audacity he had ever seen. To call him stupid before his face without his knowledge and with not so much as a flicker of her eyelids. It made him laugh to think of it. But the man *was* stupid if he thought he could endear himself to the French this way. No, it appeared this woman was in need of a rescue from death by boredom at the hands of her tiresome chaperon.

Sophie. That was what the English *imbécile* had called her.

"*Regarde ça!*"

Armand's eager voice sounded at his side, and Basile reluctantly pulled his stare away from the charming *Anglaise* inside of Stohrer's. In the vicomte's hand was a garnet brooch with gold sprays springing from its jeweled center in all directions like spindly arms of a starfish.

"You spent a half hour in the shop and contented yourself with one brooch? You amaze me. I had been sure you would have purchased half the boutique," Basile said with a lurking smile as he met Grégoire's gaze.

"Well, you see, Apolline and I have only just met," Armand said naïvely. "I should not wish to scare her off by too grand a gesture."

"You are very wise," Grégoire assured him and held out his elbow for Basile to take so they might carry on their path down the street. But Basile had already turned back to the object of his interest and was forced to step aside to allow the Englishman to exit the *pâtisserie*. Following him was the charming Englishwoman whose expression remained obscure. Had one not heard her *réplique*, one might have imagined her spiritless.

On impulse, he swept off his hat, extended his leg, and bowed before the woman, who greeted the gesture with a startled glance. Before she could protest, he spoke to her in rapid French.

"*Madame*, I beg you will forgive me the forwardness of my address when we have not been presented, but I could not help but wonder if you wished to be rescued from your stupid escort or whether you are bound through the ties of marriage and therefore beyond the hope of deliverance. Behold in me"—he bowed again—"your *chevalier*, should you need it."

The lady's face tinged with pink as her eyes widened in surprise. She opened her lips as though to answer, but none appeared ready on her tongue. The Englishman turned to see who had dared to address her and frowned.

"What is this, Sophie? I say, sir—"

Armand had been watching Basile curiously and he now stepped forward. "Have no fear of improper address, madame," he added in French, gallantly coming to Basile's aid. His friend must have sniffed an opportunity to encourage romance. "May I present Monsieur Basile Gervain, *Marquis de* Verdelle in Champagne. If you attend the salons here in Paris or even in Versailles, you may meet him everywhere. Quite unexceptionable, Monsieur Gervain."

The Englishwoman turned now to Armand, before replying in flawless French, a smile lurking in her eyes. "He is your friend, then?"

Armand bowed low before her. "I have that honor, madame."

The lady nodded graciously as though one stranger

vouching for another was a common occurrence. She brought her regard back to Basile. "It is *Mademoiselle* Twisden, and although I am quite able to rescue myself, I appreciate your concern."

"Sophie, it is not a proper thing to speak to strangers on the street." The Englishman was clearly struggling to follow what was being said and allowed his irritation to show. "I must remind you that as an English lady, you will certainly be prey to whatever designs they may have upon you." He juggled the packages from Stohrer into one hand and reached for the sword at his side, but this was done with more show than fire. He did not appear as one eager for battle. Or one capable of it.

Basile bit back a grin—rarely was he so diverted—and addressed the man in perfect, although faintly accented English. "Why sir, we in France do not propose duels to chance-met strangers. You might crush your delicious pastries." He bowed and introduced himself. "I was reminding Sophie that we had already met in London and that I was pleased to discover her here in my own country."

"Met?" The Englishman turned an astonished look to Sophie. "Where in London? Did you give him leave to use your Christian name?"

A tiny furrow appeared in Sophie's brow, then disappeared as fast. "Oh...why, we were introduced at Lady Betteridge's *al fresco* picnic, and our mutual friends insisted we all dispense with formality." Sophie smiled at Basile. "Was that not so?" A quick wit this one.

"Indeed," Basile responded, meeting the Englishman's gaze with an innocent expression before turning it back to the charming Sophie. "Well, this is chance-met. Now that you are in Paris, I hope to accord you the same welcome you gave me. How long have you been here?"

"We arrived yesterday." Sophie's eyes held an amused expression that delighted him. She was not an easy one to overset. It only confirmed his knowledge that he rarely made mistakes in his gambles.

"*Quelle chance pour moi!*" What a lucky stroke. They had crossed the line from strangers to acquaintances, and he might flirt with ease. He would continue in English now that he had secured her interest right from under the nose of her escort.

"Madame Dubigny is sending invitations to her card party tomorrow night, and I know several Englishmen who will be in attendance—along with everyone of note in Paris. I will make sure to procure an invitation for you both. Where might I send them?"

"10 rue des Saints," Sophie replied promptly. "I am staying in the lower rooms with my grandmother. And Mr. Cholmsley here, who has agreed to be our escort in Paris, is residing at Number 12."

"I do not know that we will be free tomorrow night," the Englishman replied primly. "We must visit the English embassy and see to our own acquaintances here. I believe Mr. Charles Arlington, diplomatic *attaché* to the ambassador, will be expecting our visit."

"Charles will be at the party. He told me so himself," Basile replied urbanely. "You may be sure to meet him there."

Mr. Cholmsley's furrowed brows showed how little he liked this ready answer, but before he could speak, Sophie accepted his invitation.

"I am quite sure my grandmother, Mrs. Elizabeth Twisden, and I will be delighted to attend. She has not been in Paris for many years, and must still have acquaintances who will be glad to meet her again. If this event is as grand as you say, she must certainly be well-placed to rekindle friendships there."

Basile gave her the full force of his regard as he nodded. "I, for one, shall be delighted to make your grandmother's acquaintance and will include an invitation for... Mrs. Twisden, you said?" Sophie nodded, and he went on. "I believe I had not met her in London. It was your...mother that I'd had the privilege to meet, was it not?"

The Englishman frowned. "Sophie—"

She hastened to reply in French with a strained smile. "You would not have met my mother for she died at my birth. And before you bring up my father, he died three years ago as well. I have only my grandmother."

"No," Basile corrected himself as though suddenly remembering. "It could not have been your mother. An older companion? My memory does not serve."

"Sophie," the Englishman said again, more imperatively.

She smiled and curtsied. "It must have been my friend's mother, Mrs. Vance. It was lovely to see you again, Basile." Mr. Cholmsley turned away to march forward, and she had only time to give Basile an impish grin before following her escort down the street.

He watched her go, her trim figure trailing the Englishman's. She turned her head to the side as a carriage rode by, giving a glimpse under her bonnet of tiny curls on a slender neck. Grégoire cleared his throat next to him. "What's this game, Gervain? *Ma foi*, in all the years I've known you, I've never seen you accost a pretty stranger on the street. I take it you don't know her?"

"Not yet," Basile replied, waiting until... *Oui!* She turned back to look at him, giving him a glimpse of her charming face that now showed a hint of shyness. He had hoped she might look back. "But if I must be *convoqué* to Paris to pay homage to our most dear Louis XV, only to stand on its sweltering streets until I receive permission to return to my *domaine*, I might as well amuse myself."

He accepted Greg's arm who had moved forward placidly while Armand made an unsuccessful attempt to put Basile to the blush about having fallen in love at last. The three of them moved at their own rhythm, and shopkeepers and crowds alike stepped aside to make room, even when a line of carriages tightened the space and forced the crowd against the building's façade.

Amuse myself. Basile pondered the idea. It had been some time since he had flirted with an Englishwoman. They were so proper, and it was entertaining to coax them out of their reticence.

Something tells me I will.

CHAPTER 2

Sophie bore with Sheldon's diatribe on the impertinence of the entire French race on the way back to their lodgings. She had not thought it a considerable distance when they had decided to walk to the other bank of the Seine to try this notable *pâtisserie*, but she had not crossed three streets before she wished him elsewhere.

Hm! What was the name of the attractive Frenchman, again? M. Basile Germain? No—Gervain. Of course it would be astonishing if she'd had any wits to spare after the way he singled her out with those clear blue eyes that seemed to stare straight into a person. His eyes were as blue as the waters of Cornwall. Whatever had possessed him to address *her* like that? She, who must be considered a nobody in Paris where she had no connections. He had spoken of rescuing her in that teasing way of his. Had he heard her irreverent slip of the tongue when referring to Sheldon as stupid, which she should *not* have done? It was ill-bred of her, she knew.

A lady never reveals her true feelings and never allows her composure to slip for an instant. Her governess might have left the post two years prior, but her oft-repeated words were firmly embedded in Sophie's conscience.

"I hope you are not thinking of attending that card party the foreigner spoke of." Sheldon's sudden switch from cataloging the peculiar manners of the French to his direct interrogation regarding this one in particular pierced her mental wanderings.

"If my grandmother wishes to attend, I will, of course, accompany her." This was the safest reply.

"You are not likely to receive an invitation," was his sure retort. "The event is tomorrow night, and this Madame Duby-something does not know us."

"Basile is a marquis." Sophie's outward shrug hid her private amusement at owning to the stranger's intimacy as though it were real. "He will likely achieve what he desires."

"You never mentioned having any acquaintances in Paris when we planned this trip." They crossed in front of the imposing edifice of St. Eustache church just as the bells began to ring, their deep clangs chiming from the belfry.

His tone had turned petulant the way it did whenever he felt himself thwarted. Sheldon Cholmsley had an unaccountably high opinion of his own worth and could not imagine that someone might not be in perfect accord with him on all points. He had always been a familiar figure in their house as a favorite of her father's, and she knew her grandmother was beholden to him for escorting them to Paris. If only her grandmother did not frequently cause Sophie's throat to close by encouraging a *match*, she might be able to laugh off his inflated self-importance. As it was, their nearly week-long travel together to reach Paris had only served to convince Sophie that she would not—*could not*—choose a life yoked to this man, even compared to one that bordered on destitution.

"To own the truth," Sophie answered at last, "he left London shortly after our acquaintance, and I understood he was headed for Scotland, so I did not look for him here."

If this conversation were to continue, it would tax Sophie's imagination. It was harmless, really. The marquis had tossed a ball her way in a game she did not understand, and she was merely tossing it on. Something was needed to make the summer heat and Sheldon Cholmsley more bearable.

Mercifully, their conversation drifted to safer ground, and when they finally reached their lodgings, Sophie was relieved to bid him farewell. She assured him her grandmother must still be resting and that it was not opportune to prolong their time together. She entered their rented rooms, situated on the ground floor of the terraced house. It was not as large as the one next door that Sheldon was occupying, but she found it vastly more charming. The cool air greeted her as soon as she stepped out of the sun into the dim entryway. She untied her flat *bergère* straw hat and set it on the caned chair near the entrance.

"Grandmama?"

Her voice echoed, and she heard a rustling movement from the bedroom on the far end of the house. The wooden soles of her shoes sounded on the stone floor as she traversed the corridor, her eyes on the picturesque garden visible through the glass door at the far end. She turned from the corridor to one of the bedrooms, where her grandmother was resting. Mrs. Twisden, typically indomitable despite her advanced age, portrayed a wilted appearance as she sat in the armchair. She greeted her granddaughter with a faint smile.

"Are you better for having rested?" Sophie sat on the side of her grandmother's bed nearest to the chair, her green skirt spilling out on either side of her. She lifted one of the two packages she had collected from Sheldon. "And despite your assurance that you wished for nothing, I knew as soon as I laid eyes on the *babas* that I could not return home without one for you."

"Bring that round table here," her grandmother said, her eyes on the wrapped package. "And see if Mary has returned from her attempt to buy provisions. She went out to try to purchase a few things, although she said they would not understand one word she spoke, nor she them."

Sophie set the two wrapped pastries on the bed—their accommodations might be charming, but they were small—and dragged the three-legged table over in front of her grandmother. Then she placed the two packages on top of it and tweaked the ribbon.

"I don't believe Mary has returned, for there was no noise coming from the kitchen. However, I know just as well as she does how to heat water, provided the fire is still burning. I shall fetch us some tea and plates."

Sophie did not wait for her grandmother's reply, but went into the kitchen, where she easily brought water to a boil and set out the tea things as the sounds of Mary's arrival reached her.

"Oh miss, let me help you with that." The maid set down her bundle of purchases, including vegetables and a chicken in need of plucking, continuing in a pleasant monologue about how the French were not so bad in their own way. One only had to point to things and they understood each other very well.

Sophie contributed her mite, thinking with wry amusement that Mary had fared better than Sheldon in that regard. But then, she supposed it really had to do with one's decision to make the attempt. That and a jot of humility.

Mary lifted the tray of tea and brought it into the bedroom, clucking over Sophie's persistence in bringing a third plate for her to try the French cake. She could not have persuaded Sheldon to waste his sous on a pastry that would be "cast away on a mere servant" but then neither she nor her grandmother ate so much they would be reluctant to share. The only thing Mary did insist upon was to enjoy her tea and pastry in the kitchen so she might think about how she would set up her domain for the three months they were to remain in Paris.

When it was just the two of them, Sophie recounted her walk with Sheldon, detailing where they had been and what they had seen, with her grandmother interrupting the recital with recollections and questions. She neatly left out all mention of striking up conversations with strange men, no matter how charming the man was.

"Sheldon does not appear to be any nearer to desiring to learn the French language than when we first set foot on the shores of Calais," Sophie observed with a smirk that she hid in her teacup. "He practically yelled at the tradeswoman in Stohrer, hoping that an increase in the volume of his voice might bring about her sudden fluency in the English tongue."

Her grandmother set her spoon down and allowed a contented smile to settle on her face as she savored the cake. But she had not missed the censure in Sophie's tone.

"I must say, this is as delicious as I had remembered it. Sophie, I am well aware that you view the notion of marriage to Sheldon Cholmsley with less than enthusiasm, but I hope you will consider the matter wisely."

When her grandmother stopped short, courtesy forced Sophie to prod her to continue.

"We are in somewhat straitened circumstances, and… well, we would not have been able to visit Paris without his help. It was the height of kindness for him to escort us here, though he has little love of travel, and allow me to see my beloved city before I die."

"Grandmama, please do not talk in such a way," Sophie could not help but interject. "I hope it will be many more years before such a thing occurs."

"We shall see," Mrs. Twisden said, not to be deterred. "You have inherited a house, but not a large enough income to live comfortably in it. I do not wish for you to discover what poverty is like. And although you are a girl with a lively personality which, I suppose, little accords with Sheldon's sober nature, I believe you will not find a life of scarcity to your liking."

"I suppose you are right," Sophie replied to an argument she was hearing not for the first time. She exhaled. "We may be invited to a card party by Madame Dubigny tomorrow night. Would you care to go?"

Her grandmother glanced at her sharply. "Dubigny? I believe I know her. How did you come by this invitation?"

"Oh," Sophie stalled. She would not lie to her grandmother if she could help it, but it was awkward. "We met the Marquis de Verdelle. A Monsieur Gervain it was, and he promised to have invitations sent."

By some small miracle, her grandmother did not request how they came by the introduction when they knew no one in Paris, but continued to wonder whether the Mme Dubigny was not the former Mademoiselle Paineaux. And were that indeed the case, whether she might not be assured of meeting friends from those early days before she had married Mr. Twisden and permanently retired from the Paris scene. The reminiscence caused her grandmother to brighten, and her conversation took on a decidedly more cheerful tone. Later, she came to the table for dinner, although *en déshabille* with a loose dressing gown, in a further sign of hope that anticipation of their first invitation had brought her strength back in force.

Sophie supposed she should have been surprised that the invitations to Madame Dubigny's party did indeed come that evening, but somehow when Mary opened the door to a visitor bearing the gilded cards she was not. It only confirmed her idea that M. Gervain was a resourceful man. She couldn't help but grow eager to meet him again.

The next day, Mrs. Twisden showed slight signs of being unwell. When Sophie helped her grandmother up, she found her warm to the touch. Given this development, she thought it unwise for them to attend the party. However, her grandmother refused to be deterred and Sophie hadn't the heart to insist. Mrs. Twisden was now sure Berthe Paineaux was indeed the Madame Dubigny, for she recalled the circumstances of her friend's betrothal and even recognised the address on the invitation. It did not matter how low she might be feeling, nothing for the world would allow her to miss seeing her old friend again.

Sheldon had begrudgingly agreed to attend, particularly when he had gone to the embassy that afternoon and had there discovered the ambassador himself would go. It was close enough to walk, except that Sophie did not wish to subject her grandmother to the fatigue of it and requested Sheldon to have his hired horses put to.

Her grandmother had donned a pale lilac gown that lent her a youthful air, but from what Sophie could catch from her soft mutterings, she seemed to be somewhat fearful of appearing old. As for Sophie, she wore one of the pretty gowns her grandmother had commissioned for her before they'd left London. She had not thought they would have the means for a new wardrobe, but her grandmother had surprised her. There was nothing like a becoming gown to fill a girl's heart with happy anticipation. Her evening dress was of a dark pink rose color with white laces criss-crossing above the stomacher, and the paler pink underskirt was patterned with white flowers. *Would she appear as fashionable as the French?* That was her main preoccupation.

That, and...would the marquis find it becoming?

Upon their arrival, a *majordome* ushered them into a drawing room full of people, who all turned to stare at them.

The first thing Sophie noticed was the absence of color in the room. It brought her grandmother up short, who must have noticed the same thing. The people turned toward them were clothed in blacks and the darkest of grays. Why, of course! The late king had only been dead these six weeks—much more recent than their months spent preparing for the voyage, making up all the fashionable gowns such a journey would require. There had been little evidence of mourning on their journey to the capital, but here in the glittering crowd of the *noblesse* and the *gentilhommes*, they must of course don their blacks. Sophie did not read direct censure on their faces, but she felt it all the same.

It appeared her grandmother did as well, for as Sophie took her arm, she felt the flush of heat. In another instant, Madame Dubigny moved forward to greet them with a smile. Mrs. Twisden curtsied and was already murmuring her excuses for their lapse in etiquette, but her friend brushed it off in her delight at being reunited after so many long years.

Sophie allowed her gaze to roam the crowd as the older women spoke. Adjacent to the large drawing room were two other decently sized rooms where guests were already seated to games of cards, and those in view had turned to look at her too. Embarrassing as it was to stick out so sorely, there was nothing to do now but put up a bold front or turn tail and run. Sheldon, the most ostentatious of them all in an impossibly shiny yellow satin, cleared his throat and moved with purpose toward someone he recognized from the embassy. She felt the relief of his departure immediately.

Then, a hand was at her elbow, and the marquis was bowing at her side, his deep blue eyes more compelling than she had remembered. Her heart decided an accelerated rhythm was called for.

"Sophie, I have been hoping you would come so we might renew our acquaintance."

"Our long acquaintance," she murmured with the lift of an eyebrow, calming her first reaction of pleasure to more subdued levels.

He laughed. "Of course. It has been an age. You look as lovely as you always did."

His impertinence knew no bounds, but she could only be thankful for the diversion of it. Behavior she must shun in London, she could not in Paris. Her voyage had been one of quiet suffering as Sheldon had claimed increasing intimacy by taking her arm and dogging her steps wherever she went. Basile gifted her with the ability to laugh at convention, to be pleased, and she welcomed its freedom. Besides that, it seemed to shield her from the scrutiny of the French society gathered for the card party as people began to turn their attention elsewhere.

She leaned in and murmured, "I should have noticed that you and your friends were wearing mourning clothes yesterday and taken the hint. We arrived in Paris only the day before that."

"The black serves to draw the heat, but it is unavoidable." He waved his fingers for a servant to bring a glass of something for her to drink. It was a cold, light Chablis that refreshed without being too strong.

"In truth, the king's death is the only reason I have come to Paris. Otherwise, I would be at my home in the Champagne region." He bowed again, a practiced gallantry that he softened with a wink. "But then I should not have had the felicity of meeting you."

She smiled at his empty compliment and shook her head, switching suddenly to English. "I have been wondering what had prompted you to seek the acquaintance. I can only guess some sort of a lark?"

"A lark—a bird?" He drew his brows together, and with his dark features and clear eyes focused on her, only appeared more handsome.

She lifted her chin as she smiled, determined to keep up the flirtation and not let him know how much his steady regard caused her nerves to stretch taut.

"A lark as in a game."

He smiled, his teeth impossibly white, then stepped closer to her, causing her nerves to spring loose. She was enveloped in the scent he wore. Spices—but not of the heavy sweet kind, which she despised. She could not explain it to herself. He broke all proper boundaries and all physical barriers, but he was not dangerous. She could sense he was not. There was a sweetness to his smile.

"Yes, *ma chère* Sophie. It was a game, but I mean you no harm, I assure you. You seemed too lovely to be chained to that *balourd*—forgive me."

"Forgiven," she replied promptly. "Were he less imposing upon my peace, I should be more generous with my patience."

"Monsieur Gervain, do introduce me to your lovely English companion."

It was a light feminine voice that had spoken, and Sophie turned her eyes to a young woman, who presented a stunning tableau, from her black gown with white trim to her bright blue eyes and white powdered hair. On her, the somber color was dramatic. She looked ravishing, and Sophie reminded herself to leave off flirting with the marquis in her presence or come off looking the fool. This woman was his match—*she* was not.

"Mademoiselle Zoé Sainte-Croix, allow me to present you to Mademoiselle Sophie Twisden, an Englishwoman whose acquaintance I am delighted to rekindle after an absence of two years."

Sophie's smile faltered for only an instant. She did not wish for her grandmother to get wind of the falsehood she had, on impulse, allowed to continue. Mrs. Twisden surely would if the introductions continued in this way.

"You may as well address each other by Zoé and Sophie," he went on, "since I have a feeling we are going to be in frequent company this summer, and there is nothing more tedious than *Mademoiselle Ceci* and *Mademoiselle Cela.*"

Sophie hesitated. To address each other by their given names would be to claim instant friendship with a woman she did not know—and one who was more likely to capture the marquis' heart than she was. But then, what did she have to lose in this foreign city? It was not like the marquis was hers, anyway.

She smiled at Zoé, determined to offer unguarded friendship until the woman should otherwise prove unworthy of it. "You are most welcome to use my Christian name if it suits you. I do not mind."

Zoé returned the overture with warmth and assured her she should be only too glad and hoped to learn where she was staying so she might visit. Sophie had not yet had time to offer a reply when the sounds of Sheldon's voice from behind caused her to stiffen.

"Sophie, come. I must present you to all the Englishmen and women here."

She lifted her eyes to Basile, then Zoé, and continued in French. "As you have heard, I have been summoned. I am staying at 10 rue des Saints in the *Faubourg de Saint Germain*, and I would be delighted to receive you." Her words were directed at Zoé alone, for as much as she had forayed outside of the strictest respectability by such bold flirtation, she would not be so improper as to invite *him*.

But as she followed behind Sheldon, her thoughts became muddled. She had not realized how much she had taken a liking to the marquis until the appearance of the beautiful Frenchwoman—who was clearly on the best of terms with him—made evident how foolish she was to hold out for anything beyond a mere friendship.

CHAPTER 3

Basile watched Sophie leave, a smile playing upon his lips. He remained in place until one of the unmarried women who had foisted an introduction upon him that week caught his expression and threatened to attribute the smile to herself. He turned abruptly to find Zoé examining him.

"Lovely girl. It is about time you struck up a flirtation. You've been in Paris for a month, and all I have seen is that face of dead *ennui* you present to the world, which I know to be a masquerade."

"'Tis only that, however. A flirtation. Lest you get any ideas of the matrimonial sort." He flicked his glance at her, knowing she would not tease him over it. Their families had long been friends, and they understood one another quite well. Zoé was lovely to look upon, and despite the difference in their years, she never bored him. It was almost surprising that he had never felt anything for her beyond the most fraternal affection. But then, he supposed if he had it would mean the end to his bachelor days, and he was far from being ready for such a step. And, of course, her love of frivolity would cause her to chafe were she to be cooped up on his estate.

She scoffed. "*I* know *that*. You won't be ready for marriage until you have decided you prefer the comfort of one woman to the harassment of many." Zoé sent him a considering glance. "You have not yet realized that whatever threat the masses pose to your freedom is more burdensome than giving up your freedom willingly to the right woman."

"Have you always been so philosophical, my dear?" He took out his snuffbox and fingered the encrusted sapphires on its lid without opening it. "But as you have correctly guessed, for the moment I prefer the threat to my comfort over the threat to my liberty, which will quickly be destroyed in the matrimonial state."

Zoé turned to look at him, one hand resting on her waist above the wide *paniers*. "Still, I must ask. What was it that has caught your attention with this lovely girl? She is like any other, is she not? And Englishwomen we do have in Paris."

Basile pursed his lips and narrowed his eyes in thought. "She *is* lovely. I like the look in her eyes. Intelligent if you chance to draw her out, veiled if you don't. She has a quick wit and caught my game soon enough—"

He stopped short. He had truly not meant to spread it about that he had forced the introduction and knew he could trust Grégoire and Armand to keep mum. He supposed he could trust Zoé too.

"Game?" This came with the arch of a carefully shaped brow.

He met her gaze with a lurking smile. He would have to take her into his confidence. "She was being quelled by that English peacock over there in yellow. And she showed spirit by poking at him in French, which he could not understand. This naturally delighted me, so I pretended we were prior acquaintances. She played my ruse without blinking an eyelid."

"Basile!" Zoé said in quiet astonishment, laughter bubbling below the surface. "You have only just met her?"

"Yesterday," he admitted, then lifted his finger to his lips. "How fares your suit with our dear friend, Charles?"

Zoé turned a rosy pink underneath the white powder on her face, glancing in the gentleman's direction. "You said that entirely too loud for my liking." Her voice went lower as she leaned in. "The English are a discreet race. I know he harbors feelings for me, but unlike warm-blooded Frenchmen who accost perfect strangers on the street, he does not admit it. I am not even sure he will admit it to himself."

Basile glanced over at the Englishman who seemed to be entrapped in conversation by the peacock. He allowed his eyes to rest on them long enough for Charles to feel he was being watched and to throw a glance their way. His eyes went immediately to Zoé and his color rose.

Basile didn't miss it. "He likes you, *ma chérie*. I have a feeling you will be Mrs. Arlington before long. You need only be patient."

She sniffed. "I am patient." When he swallowed a snort of laughter she turned to him and gave him a prim look. "You shall see. I will not even go near him. I *am* patient."

She proceeded to do exactly as she'd promised, and Basile watched Charles's stare follow her as she flitted from one man to another, using every art of coquetry she possessed. If he was reading the man correctly, Zoé was not playing the game of flirtation in a way most suited to her target.

He turned his eyes back to Sophie who had been brought into conversation by the wife of one of the ambassador's staff. By now, Cholmsley had made his way to her side and was forcing both women to listen with polite interest. Ah, it looked like another rescue was in order, and why not? It was the only interesting thing he could find to do in a city that bored him dreadfully. As Marquis de Verdelle, he was obliged to stay in Paris for some months and show his royal support along with the other *noblesse* and *courtisans*. But—*que diantre!*—it was what he liked least of all. He was never meant to be the marquis.

That one might lose an eldest brother to a childhood illness was a thing to be deplored but perfectly understandable, and one hardly recalled his face to mind for it was so long ago. That the next brother in line might depart this world by attempting a swim in an unfamiliar pond while under the influence of a bottle or two of Bordeaux was certainly a shocking thing that must send the entire family into a spiral of grief. But that the third in line must sink in the middle of the Atlantic Ocean in a most unfittingly named ship, *Felicity*, while returning to take up the family mantle was to suffer too cruelly under Fate's hand.

He was never meant to be the marquis.

"Claudia Bordenave has returned to Paris at last and is here." Grégoire came to stand at Basile's side, careful not to look at the woman in question. He knew the danger of it.

Basile hid his scowl but was not able to temper the mixture of anger and longing that rose up in him and which irritated him with its potency. He had been fooled by Claudia once. She was like wolfsbane. Beautiful in appearance but with roots that were poisonous. As a young man on the town, he had been seduced by her beauty, too naïve to see it went no deeper than what one could see. She was a favorite of Madame Du Barry, the former king's mistress, and under her guidance Claudia soon broke their engagement to marry more advantageously.

While he'd been heartbroken when she had withdrawn her affection to marry a wealthy man who was older than her father, he soon came to realize his lucky escape. She had been no more faithful to her husband or her vows than she had been to Basile. And now she had been pursuing him relentlessly ever since her widowhood aligned with his succession to the title.

Out of the corner of his eye, he saw the sudden shift in her profile and her deliberate steps forward. Claudia was petite and possessed the most elegant figure he had ever seen with a tiny, nipped waist, and a generous bosom that was set to advantage by revealing much of it. Underneath her rich chestnut locks that were always powdered fashionably white she possessed beguiling almond-shaped eyes and full, pouting lips. She was fully conscious of her assets and never shy about bringing them into close proximity of gentlemen who might admire them.

"*Mon cher* Basile. How good it is to see you in Paris again."

"Madame Bordenave." Basile offered her a polite bow and turned back to Grégoire to take up their engrossing conversation which they'd had no time to begin.

"You are determined to snub me," she said. "But we are old friends, are we not? You cannot think I am so easily discouraged." Her lighthearted laugh seemed designed to let him know how little she cared that he remained aloof. Basile would have to be more obvious.

"As such old friends, we hardly need stand on ceremony. Therefore, I am sure you will not expect me to dog your footsteps all night. I should not dream of chasing away your suitors." Basile gave her a bland smile and turned his back on her.

"I see the English Miss Sophie has come after all." Grégoire pronounced Miss like *mees* as he nodded in that direction.

"Of course she has," Basile replied, still aware of Claudia's presence at his side and eager to cut short any further attempts on her part. He slipped his arm through Grégoire's and led him away as though in search of refreshments, his eyes on Sophie. She looked patently bored, a feeling he himself could not bear. "But I fear I may be called upon to intervene. 'Tis a tragedy that she should have to suffer the man's conversation for lack of protectors. The sight offends."

"I shall not deter you, then. So long as I shall not be called upon to take her place with the English gentleman." Grégoire gave the ghost of a smile and moved away from Basile, easily joining another group of soberly clad courtiers who were the latest to receive the queen's favor and who were no doubt there to bring her the latest gossip.

Basile made his decision and moved forward. He reached the two out of three brightly dressed guests in the whole room and held out his arm to Sophie.

"You must permit me to present you to Madame Lengard. She is another such hostess as Madame Dubigny who entertains all of Paris. I thought to procure an invitation for you to attend her event on Thursday."

Sophie's bright, expressive eyes met his for a moment and she turned her attention to her companion, who was frowning. Basile could see hesitation in her eyes, but she was already moving over to take his arm. He threw out a salve to the man's dignity.

"I shall, of course, request that Madame Lengard

provide you with an invitation as well, *monsieur*." He bowed to Mr. Cholmsley and carried away his partner without any compunction over leaving him alone in a crowd of people he scarcely knew and whose language he did not speak.

"You must have a keen eye for my anguish, for you have rescued me again." Sophie sent him a warm look of gratitude that one might almost mistake for admiration to one less cool-headed than he. Armand would have already been planning another trip to the *boutique du bijoutier* for a brooch.

"I cannot help but do so, for I am a man who upholds the law." He led her neatly into a space near the wall where there were fewer people to interrupt their *tête-à-tête*.

"The law?" She smiled at him, the tiny frown lines between her eyes betraying her confusion.

"'Tis a crime that someone as charming as you should be forced to listen to an *homme sans intérêt* such as he."

She laughed. "'Tis true, he is not the most interesting of men. I can scarcely conceal my yawns when I am with him. It is most ill-bred of me, for"—she lifted her forefinger as though instructing—"a lady should make the most uninteresting companion feel as though his conversation were enlightening."

"Who says such a thing? Do you?" Basile kept her arm in his and allowed himself to stand as near to her as he liked. It did no one any harm, for he knew the rules in Paris were not the same as in London. Besides, she smelled of oranges. It was the most refreshing scent in a room full of cloves and patchouli liberally applied to mask the less pleasant odors.

"I do not. 'Twas my governess, who had many such maxims. I can quote them all."

She glanced at him smiling and pulled away a fraction

when their eyes met. As for Basile, he had not expected the clip to his chest when he met her gaze and could understand why she had pulled away. It was a foreign sensation to be so instantly attracted to a lady and not an emotion he was ready to devote much thought to.

"I believe you might leave your governess's maxims aside while in Paris, particularly when suffering under the attention of an overly interested admirer. Here we prefer to say as Molière taught us: 'If this be your way to love, I beg you will hate me.'"

Sophie laughed, then raised her fingers to her lips and choked it back. Several people turned their way, including Madame Filbert, whose attention he was careful to avoid as she had two daughters she wished to marry off. Her eyes glittered with interest at the sight of him, and he nodded before pivoting slightly with Sophie so she was not in direct view.

Sophie's eyes smiled, Basile decided, even as her lips resumed their natural position. She was too vibrant a woman to be chained to a man such as the peacock.

"Why do you accept the company of the p—the Englishman? I have forgotten his name." Basile waved away its importance. "You must surely have friends whose company would delight you more. An English suitor?" He smiled but with less delight at the thought. He could not see Sophie with a man whose blood ran thinly in his veins.

"Ah, yes, Mr. Cholmsley." Her arm was still in his, and she slipped it from his elbow then unfurled her fan and began to wave it. "Alas, my grandmother wishes for the match. I will not hide from you that whatever fortune my family once had, it is now a mere pittance. She hopes to save me from poverty."

Sophie glanced at him with a wan smile. "It is more

honesty than you would wish for perhaps, but at least you will never be able to accuse me of setting my sights above my station."

The answering smile came naturally to Basile. How unusual this woman was! "I own, I find your honesty refreshing."

Sophie hid her smile behind her fan—in shyness, he thought, rather than coquetry. "Very well."

"Have you another project dear to your heart if you are to escape marriage to him? Do you hope to marry someone else?"

The words were out, and her expression carried a most pointed application, which gave him his answer. It filled him with chagrin—a most unusual feeling for him.

I must be out of my mind to talk this way. There is only one answer a woman can give you, and you are leading her to hope in vain that you are her savior and solution. Fortunately, Sophie Twisden did not seem a woman to cling to a fruitless endeavor.

"I suppose I prefer almost anything to marrying Sheldon." Her voice had dropped to a whisper. "I am ready to take on any position that might spare me this fate. But he has been pressing his advantage, and I believe he hopes to secure a promise before our trip is at its end. This is, of course, most uncomfortable, since he is our escort in Paris and my grandmother and I are entirely at his mercy. I have been holding him off."

"Allow me to encourage you to remain strong." Basile lifted her hand and placed it back on his arm. "It would be the greatest tragedy to succumb for lack of friends."

"Oh, are we friends now?" she asked lightly. He thought it cost her, for her smile wavered almost imperceptibly.

"Why, we have been friends these past two years, my

dear Sophie." He looked at her in feigned astonishment and was delighted to see the ready laughter return to her lips.

Just as he decided to relinquish her to her grandmother's care so as not to draw too much speculation over their attachment—or raise any hope in her breast—the peacock moved toward them at what must have been an accelerated pace for him. She raised her eyes, just as Mr. Cholmsley flagged her attention.

"Sophie, come. We must leave straight away. Your grandmother is unwell."

"Oh!" Sophie's expression changed in an instant as all humor and pleasantry left it. "Forgive me. I must attend to her."

"Yes, of course. I wish her a quick convalescence." Basile caught sight of the older woman being helped to the door. Attending the party so soon on the heels of the older woman's arrival in Paris must have been too taxing.

Sophie left him without a second glance or anything else that might lead him to believe she would unwittingly develop any sort of *tendresse* for him that might ruin their delightful discourse. It was all the better that she did not. Still, it was a shame she must be consigned to the boring Englishman's care, both tonight and during her stay in Paris.

CHAPTER 4

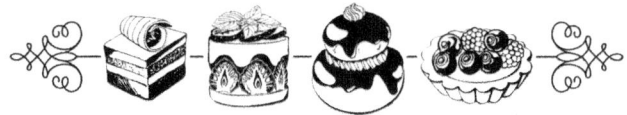

Mrs. Twisden was roused from a troubled slumber to receive the doctor's second visit since she'd fallen ill. After she had submitted to his ministrations, the doctor met Sophie outside of her grandmother's room. His grave expression caused her heart to seize.

"Well, Monsieur Pichon, how is my *grand-mère*?"

He shook his head soberly, then adjusted his wig. "She has caught an inflammation of the lungs, which is injurious for a woman of any age and may prove fatal at hers. I believe you should begin making preparations."

She stared at him blankly, and though she refused to understand his meaning, her limbs grew cold. "Preparations?"

"It is always wise to prepare for the worst, mademoiselle." He reached for the hat that Mary handed him and put it on his head. "At a time when a nation's king falls ill and dies, it very often provokes a like-minded response in the more sensitive of women. Their very natural outpouring of grief will take on a more sinister form, leading to an unhappy ending."

"I assure you, Monsieur Pichon, my grandmother is suffering from no such thing. She has only arrived in Paris the day before yesterday." Sophie followed him to the door, unable to keep the astringency from her reply.

"Ah, with her level of French so superior—and yours as well. I had thought… But then it was certainly her journey that has fatigued her to the point of ill health. As I have already advised, you would do well to make preparations for the worst."

That was enough. Sophie welcomed the anger that rose up against his morbid predictions, for she could not bear to succumb to fear. Her grandmother simply *must* come through this.

She offered the doctor a tight smile by way of answer and held the door for him to leave, waving Mary away. She wanted to be the one to put the harbinger of gloom firmly on the other side of it.

"Can you believe this man?" she asked Mary as soon as he had left. "Much good his learning has done him if all he can do is to put on a long face and attempt no remedy that doesn't involve cupping."

"I could see you were not best pleased, miss, but as I can make out nothing of what he says…it is only a bunch of gibble-gabble to me. What *did* the sawbones say?"

"It is not worth repeating, but I shall have to find another doctor nearby. Or wanting that, an apothecary." She clenched her fists tight. "Oh, but it is frustrating to be in a foreign city when there is a particular need—and I with limited means in finding a solution."

A knock sounded on the door, and Mary went past her to open it. It occurred to Sophie a moment too late that it would likely be Sheldon, the very last person she wished to see.

"Ah, Mary. Here is my hat. Sophie." Sheldon glided forward and held her hand firmly in his, patting it and offering her a fulsome look, which caused his chin to quiver. She slipped her hand from his, accepting the inevitable.

"Please, join me in the sitting room. Mary, you may bring us some tea, if you please."

The maid dipped a curtsy for Sheldon's sake and disappeared, leaving Sophie to entertain her unwelcome visitor.

When he had settled himself comfortably, he looked around the room with a critical air at the simple furnishings. Then he turned to meet her regard. "What did *Moesyur* Pichon say?"

"The most outlandish thing," she retorted, her fire returning at the memory. "He said to prepare for the worst." She clamped her lips shut to ward off the inexplicable urge to cry. "Grandmama is unwell, but it's just a slight fever and cough, for heaven's sake. I would much rather he bring her medicine than offer a lugubrious prognosis."

"Ah, but Sophie, you can know nothing of the matter. Although he is French, he is a doctor—and a man—and as such must have more knowledge of her true situation than you could guess at. I am sure you might trust what he says."

After a quick glance at the open door and the empty corridor beyond it, he turned his gaze back to her. "I know we have not yet discussed the matter openly, but I believe we should announce our betrothal early on in our stay in Paris to avoid confusion. I've seen the way that French marquess thinks to make you the object of his attention, and it would be well for him to know you are already spoken for."

Betrothal? Sophie's eyes grew large, and she could feel the color shoot up to her hairline. "I beg your pardon, but there is no betrothal to announce, for you have not asked but only hinted, and I have certainly given you neither a positive answer, nor even encouragement."

"Ah." He leaned forward on the chair, and in doing so managed to encroach upon her space without being within arm's length.

"Then let me waste no time in making my intentions clear, Sophie. I have expressed them often enough to your grandmother and have found her receptive to the idea. Therefore, *you* could surely have no objections." He planted his elbows on his knees and opened his palms. "Naturally, I assumed you and she had spoken of it and that the matter was understood, but that your maidenly sensitivity hindered you from revealing your own wishes."

Sophie stood, causing Sheldon to scramble to his feet. "I assure you my maidenly sensitivity would not lead me to offer you false hope. My grandmother has spoken of her wishes to see me avoid a life of reduced means by entering into an advantageous match. But she knows—for I have told her—that I cannot entertain the notion of an alliance where my affections are not engaged."

Sheldon frowned and a sudden flush caused his pointed nose to turn red. "Choosing to marry for affection is not something I hold to, you must know. It is a modern notion and has nothing to recommend it. Marriage is best brought about when a man has thought through the advantages and draws up the contract with a sober and steady mind."

At this, Sophie's lip twitched. Despite the dreadful timing of the proposal and her worry for her grandmother, the complete lack of finesse by her would-be intended provoked an inappropriate desire to laugh. It was either that or burst into a fit of melancholy, and she had no wish to appear weak. She took a brief moment to marshal her thoughts before the obvious struck her.

"But what do you hope to gain from the match, Sheldon? You say you enter into it with a cool head, but you know very well I bring no dowry. How can you claim that this is an advantageous match for *you*? I can see none."

She seemed to have hit home a point because he looked confused for a moment. It was brief, however, before his natural pomposity regained itself. He stretched his chin up as though to loosen a constricting cravat.

"Well..." He cleared his throat. "At times, a gentleman might propose for noble reasons—to save a woman from an uncomfortable fate. That, too, is a rational decision."

"That *is* most noble, I assure you," Sophie answered, eager to make herself very clear. "Since you have proposed in such an altruistic manner, allow me to repay your kindness in the most charitable way I can. That is to reject your generous proposal for the simple reason that I feel we should not suit. To avoid further discomfort, I wish you will say no more on the topic."

"I believe your rejection is too hastily given, and you would do well to lend my proposal more consideration." Sheldon stopped short and looked toward the corridor, where Sophie heard the sounds of the tea cups being set on the tray.

She went over to shut the door. Mary would know not to enter with the door closed, and Sophie had only one objective, which was to cut short Sheldon's stay. She was soon grateful for having done so, for she would not like her grandmother to have overheard the rest.

"We are here in Paris because of my willingness to provide escort for the journey. We are both aware that you and your grandmother could not otherwise have come. I undertook this journey with the understanding that marriage was a settled thing between us, Sophie. But I must warn you, I should not be comfortable staying in this dreadful city if I learn we are not to be married after all. And you will not find it an easy thing to remain here without me, or even to return to London, without my help to ease your way."

"I am glad we understand each other," she replied, her temper rising. "You require that I marry you if I do not wish to be left completely to my own devices with Grandmama sick and few friends in the city?"

He drew himself up stiffly. "I did not quite say that. I have an esteem for your grandmother. I wish for her to be well. I will not abandon you here without offering some assistance, but I most certainly will not remain the length of our intended stay. You would do well to reflect on this before you reject my proposal in such definitive terms."

Sheldon's face was visibly red around his jowls, and he walked toward the door to the sitting room. Before he opened it, he turned back to face her with a stiff bow.

"I will bid you good day."

"Good day," Sophie mumbled, grasping at the most basic courtesy. Her fears for her grandmother, made worse by the doctor's dire prognosis, had made it difficult to greet Sheldon's unwanted and ill-timed marriage proposal with any degree of civility.

She sat suddenly as Mary brought the tray in.

"He didn't stay long."

"I encouraged his early departure," Sophie replied. "Mary, come and sit. You may share some of my tea. We are too humble a household to stand upon ceremony, and this is an unusual situation we are in, living as we do, far from England."

Mary sat quietly on the edge of the chair, clearly ill at ease with the notion, and waited while Sophie poured the tea. They each drank without speaking. Sophie was worried, and Mary was wise enough not to fill the silence with empty talk.

"Do you think my grandmother is in a very bad state?" Sophie asked her.

Mary thought for a moment, clasping her strong fingers over a worn apron. "She's not fallen ill like this before in England. I don't know if it's the dirty city we're living in or the long voyage that provoked it, but I admit to having some cause for worry."

Sophie nodded. She had attempted to force her thoughts into a more positive direction ever since she'd brought her grandmother home the night before, but she could not help but feel anxious. Her grandmother was her only family; and in some ways, Mrs. Twisden's protection and good name had kept at bay the necessity for Sophie to choose between marriage, finding a position somewhere, or settling on the small property she had inherited with scarcely the means to live upon it. For Sophie, this visit to Paris was supposed to be her last moment of lightheartedness before she would be forced to think about her future. Now, even this was being cut short in the direst way. She had not even seriously contemplated what course to follow.

Another knock sounded at the door, and Sophie shot a dark look at Mary. *Sheldon again!* He could not leave well enough alone. She put her hand up to the maid, her lips set firmly.

"No, Mary. For once, I will open the door. It is Mr. Cholmsley coming back with more well-meaning advice, and if I was too kind in my refusal before, I will not be so now. I shall send him off in no short order."

"Your grandmother won't like me drinking tea with you and sitting while you open doors. She'll think I've gone above my station, and she'll be right."

Mary's look of distress caused Sophie to soften. "I promise to be mistress of the house again. Just humor me now, for I cannot bear to have him set foot inside for the second time in one day. I will be more effective than you in refusing him admittance."

She strode out of the sitting room and into the corridor, where she opened the front door with more force than was necessary. Outside on the cobblestone street stood Basile Gervain and Zoé Sainte-Croix. Sophie's hand dropped to her side as she stared at them in surprise. Basile extended his leg and bowed, and Zoé curtsied.

At the gesture, Sophie recollected her manners and returned the curtsy, then stepped back. "Forgive me for my lack of a proper welcome. I am only surprised to see you, that is all. But won't you both come in?"

"You are very kind," Zoé replied. "I hope we are not coming at an inopportune time."

"Not at all." Sophie smiled at her and brought her eyes to Basile, touched that he had visited, fearful of what he would think of their humble lodgings. "You are both aware that my grandmother is ill, but she is resting in her room."

"Did you have a doctor come by to look at her?" Basile asked as he followed her and Zoé into the sitting room. Mary was collecting the teapot and cups, and she stopped to curtsy to the visitors before carrying them out of the room.

Sophie watched her go, somewhat at a loss for how she should entertain her guests. "It was a Monsieur

Pichon that attended to her, and I almost wish I had not had anyone come. He brought nothing in the way of medicine. At least nothing that I recognized to be beneficial. He bled her and then told me I should prepare for her funeral. If he is to be believed, there is no fear of my appearing at a *soirée* in colors again, for my entire wardrobe will need to be fitted with blacks before the week is out."

She exhaled audibly, then attempted a smile, which she knew was weak. But if she allowed herself to give way to fears, it would paralyze her for action.

The marquis raised an eyebrow. "I don't know this Monsieur Pichon, but it does not sound as though he was in the slightest bit helpful."

"He most certainly was not." Sophie realized with a start that her guests were still standing, and she gestured to the chairs in a circle around the unused fireplace. "Please have a seat."

She clutched her hands on her lap and found her fingers trembling. Her guests seemed to miss nothing and watched as she slipped her hands to the side underneath her skirts. She smiled as brightly as she could.

"May I offer you something in the way of refreshments?"

They glanced at each other before Zoé replied. "We do not wish to trespass upon your time, not with your grandmother unwell. We merely came to see how we might be of service."

"You are very kind." The gesture was just what she needed, although if Sheldon should make good on his threats, she could hardly ask them for help returning home —or to bury her grandmother should the doctor's grim words come true. "I...I think there is nothing to do at the moment, but your kind solicitation brings me great comfort."

They sat awkwardly, listening to the sounds of the clock ticking in the corner and the muffled noises in the kitchen as Mary began washing dishes. Zoé stood then, and Basile followed.

"I fear we must be on our way, but here is my card," Zoé said. "You may call upon me for anything you might need." She glanced at the marquis, who gave no immediate indication of wishing to leave. At last he nodded and brought his gaze back to Sophie.

She gestured for them to accompany her to the door. How terrible it was. She could not welcome them in a hospitable way as she would have liked. At the moment, they seemed her best hope for friendship in Paris, but with her grandmother as ill as she was, Sophie was likely doomed to spend the whole of her stay here in the apartment, coaxing her back to health. She refused to think of the possibility that her grandmother might die.

This would surely be the last time she would see the marquis and his friend. By the time her grandmother was well, they would likely have forgotten all about her.

When they reached the corridor, Mary was standing with the door open. Zoé retied her bonnet, although she had only just taken it off and stepped out onto the street. Basile turned back to Sophie and caused her heart to grow still by another one of his direct looks.

"I would send you a doctor of my acquaintance if you do not object. He has seen to my mother and sister in the past, and I believe you might trust him."

Sophie could scarcely conceal her surprise. She had suspected Basile was considerate, but as his predominant qualities were ones of humor and mischief, his kindness when it mattered spoke volumes. She managed to articulate her acceptance.

He gave a nod. "As it is late in the day, I will have Monsieur Comble come tomorrow. And then, if you will not find it incommodious, we will visit again the day afterwards to see how your grandmother fares?"

Sophie darted her eyes to Zoé, who was watching Basile with a strange look on her face. She wondered if Zoé loved him—how could she not?—or if they had some sort of an understanding. It would make sense that they did. After all, they were of the same quality, whereas Sophie's family had steadily come down in the world. She dragged her eyes back to Basile and found his still on her.

"I would be most grateful for your kind attention," she replied, forcing herself to look at them both in equal measure. She would not allow either of them to suspect that she might have even the smallest *tendre* for Basile.

Which of course she did not.

CHAPTER 5

They left Sophie's rented lodgings, and Zoé studied Basile's face as though attempting to read something of his intentions there. He would not give her cause to read too much into intentions he himself did not quite understand.

"'Tis no small thing to care for a loved family member in a foreign city. You did well to propose we come," she said.

"I suspected she would not have access to the right care, being so new to the city," he replied mildly.

In truth, the fact that he had thought about her enough to bestir himself on her behalf surprised no one more than himself. But the compulsion to see her left him with no peace until he put the idea into motion.

"She appeared calm enough, but one could see her agitation," Zoé observed. "It is why I proposed we not stay."

He had thought to find Sophie pale and listless with worry upon arrival, but instead her eyes were snapping and her cheeks aflame when she threw open the door. It was almost as though she were expecting someone else and was ready for battle. He wondered if she had been harassed by the peacock that day and mistook their visit for another unwelcome one of his. He would have to ask her.

"*You* were not inclined to stay longer, were you?" Zoé insisted.

"No, no. It was not meant to be a long visit." Basile replied, somewhat absent-mindedly. He ignored Zoé's piercing looks.

"*Eh bien*! If you don't mean to tell me any more, I suppose we must find some other *discours* to squabble over," she said in a pique.

Basile hid a smile. She was so easy to bait, even when he was not trying. "I suppose we must. How did Charles take to your ignoring him all evening?"

Zoé frowned. "It is most unaccountable, but he seems to give up so easily at the slightest resistance. I should like to see him show himself a man and fight for me."

"Ah, but perhaps you have misjudged your Englishman." Basile led Zoé along the border of the Seine, the most direct path to her house on rue Dauphine. "Some men would prefer to have your fidelity without needing to fight for it."

"Is that true?" Zoé looked at him curiously. "What about you? What would you do if you were indeed in love and your woman flirted with another man to provoke you?"

Basile was silent for a moment, his mouth turned downwards. "Why, my dear, that is entirely another matter. I would remove her from his company and waste no time in kissing her senseless until she forgot any other man existed."

"*Là*!" Zoé said, her face breaking out into a smile. "It is a shame I have not the slightest *tendresse* for you, for that is what I should like above all things. Only, I should like for it to be Charles kissing me like that."

"Rid yourself of the notion that I will drop a word in his ear. I leave you to your own affair," Basile said.

"*Pfft!*" was all Zoé gave by way of reply.

THE NEXT NIGHT, Basile went to the opera in need of some diversion, but he found the experience insipid. His box was filled with people he felt obliged to invite, but who he did not particularly wish to converse with. He went out into the foyer during the entr'acte for refreshments and Grégoire sought him there with news.

"Armand seems to have made a conquest at last, and it is not the fair Apolline of the garnet brooch."

Basile raised an eyebrow. "Indeed! And who is she?"

"She is one of Marie-Antoinette's attendants, and she blushes when he is near." Grégoire watched the crowd walk by them and nodded at one of the patrons.

"He has aimed high then," Basile said. He hoped for Armand's sake it would last.

"She is perhaps easily overlooked as one of the less-favored of the queen's attendants. But her heart seems true."

"I would not wish anything better for him," Basile said, before catching sight of the last person he wished to see, parading by in a swirl of silks. He turned suddenly in an attempt to hide his face, his anxiety increasing a notch. Would he never be rid of her? "*Fichtre!* It's La Bordenave."

But it was too late. Claudia had already seen him and cut across the crowd to where they stood.

"Why, Basile—Monsieur St. Pierre. What a delight to find you both here. The evening is growing ever more promising." She slipped her arm through Basile's, pulling him close. Her scent cloyed, and he found her grip firm when he tried to lessen the hold. "*À vrai dire*, you have only improved with age."

Grégoire shifted slightly and cleared his throat as he glanced at her, clearly at a loss for how to help Basile. The Duc de Lauzun spotted him before coming over. "St. Pierre, you've a hunter for sale, do you not? I've a mind to purchase it." With a "bonsoir" and a bow to Basile and Claudia, he hurried him off. Grégoire sent an apologetic look over his shoulder to Basile.

He extricated his arm from Claudia's, which produced a playful pout on her face. It goaded him that he could still find her attractive even without any desire to win her back. As she put every bit of art into her appearance that was naturally endowed with womanly beauty, it was also unsurprising.

"Come now, Basile," she protested. "You know you are the tiniest bit glad to see me again. Admit it."

He regarded her with narrowed eyes. "What do you want, Claudia?"

"Nothing." She shrugged and gave a laugh while fanning herself. "Everything. Why should we not pick up where we were before, but this time with both of us wiser about love? Admit it. You are holding out your heart for me. This is why you have never married."

"I have not married because I have not found the woman I wish to spend the rest of my life with." A sudden bit of devilry made him add, "Until now."

"Oh!" She turned her wide eyes to him, and he could see the surprise and hesitation in them. The speculation over whether it might be her, but common sense informing her it was not. "Do tell. Have you found your *marquise*?"

"I do not believe you are acquainted with her," he said dampeningly.

She fanned herself, her smile somewhat dimmed. After a moment she dropped her hand to her side. "I do not believe you. I think you have entirely made her up. Basile, I wish you to know that I regret not having married you when I had the chance to do so. But now, think how much I would bring to a match between us. I am as wealthy as you please and am a favorite at court."

"*Were* a favorite," he corrected. "Madame Du Barry has been sent to a convent in Meaux, and you are unlikely to curry favor with the queen."

"Come now," she retorted, her voice sharp. Taking hold of herself, she continued, now coaxing. "If you must know, the queen and I have reached a little understanding. I can be—"

"Madame, you must excuse me. I am afraid I am not interested." He gave a slight bow and left before he had to listen to any more.

IT HAD BEEN two days since Basile had seen Sophie, although he received word from the doctor who had attended to Mrs. Twisden, and who was hopeful of her prognosis. He wished to know how she fared and decided to visit, though Zoé was unable to accompany him this time. It was unclear if she was trying to promote a connection she thought he wished for, or if she truly was busy.

He was admitted by the maid this time, not by Sophie. His speculation over whether they had a male servant grew more decided. He suspected they did not.

"Miss Twisden is in the garden. I will fetch her," the maid said, but Basile held out his hand.

"I will join her in the garden, if you will show me the way." Even as he said the words, he could see the small trees and climbing plants over a trellis through the glass door at the end of the corridor. It was one of the charms of her living arrangement. The rooms might be small, but there was a full view of a beautiful green space that made the whole seem larger and brighter.

The maid curtsied and led the way to the door. When she opened it for him, he stepped through it and turned back.

"I will introduce myself. You need have no fear for your mistress." He smiled at her, and the maid curtsied again in reply before reentering the kitchen.

When he cast his gaze over the verdant space, he found it bigger than he had first thought because, while the immediate area outside the door was an immaculate garden with fruit trees and trimmed bushes, there was a wilder section farther back with trees, bushes, and stone benches. He spotted her figure from where he stood and strode forward. The day was sunny and mercifully cooler than it had been in the days past.

When he was a few feet away, she looked up and her face lit with a smile that reached her eyes. That was immediately followed by a deep blush. The view nearly stopped him in his tracks. She was charming in this bucolic setting—almost like an English country maid with rosy cheeks and simple dress, a straw basket sitting at her feet. It reminded him of his hitherto carefree days when he had been able to travel throughout England, Wales, and Scotland.

"Monsieur Gervain," she said, standing in some confusion.

"Are we back to formal address now?" he replied with a lift of an eyebrow.

"No, no, Basile. I am Sophie to you, as ever." She seemed quickly to have recovered her self-possession and smiled at him in a way he could only describe as saucy. He returned the grin.

"May I?" he asked, gesturing to the bench beside her. It was small, but there was not another one nearby and it would have to do if he did not wish to have her craning her neck up at him. She moved over by way of answer, and he was careful not to crush the skirt of her gown when he sat.

"How is your grandmother?" he asked, turning in place to catch a glimpse of her face.

She looked straight ahead, and her pinched expression gave him the answer he sought. She twiddled a stem of lavender in her fingers.

"She is quite ill, but I must thank you for sending Monsieur Comble. I find him to be a reasonable man, not giving airs that some doctors do. And he doesn't bleed his patients." She sent Basile a tremulous smile. "I discovered that you had paid for his services. He would accept nothing from me."

Basile didn't wish to dwell on that and he waved it away. "He is trustworthy. Although he is not King Louis's principal doctor, he had been called upon to consult over our recently departed king."

"Had he!" Sophie brought her wide-eyed gaze to him. "He must be a notable doctor indeed. My grandmother does seem to be coughing less after taking the treatment he prescribed."

"That is good news." Basile was silent for a moment,

enjoying the sun, the medley of flowers, and the sound of buzzing life that surrounded them. He was conscious of her skirts next to him and of the impulse to lean into her. To kiss her cheek, causing her to turn—

He stood, and Sophie looked at him in consternation before getting to her feet. "I suppose you must be going? You came only to have news?"

"Yes, to have news of your grandmother. I also wished..."

He paused as he considered again the idea that had come over him that very morning. It was impulsive, but he would do it. "I wished to send my old nurse to aid in the caring of your grandmother if you would permit it. Jeannot—it is her family name, you see—declares she is growing idle. My sister Thérèse is in the expectant way, but until there are children to dote upon, Jeannot is looking for something to fill her days. Do you suppose her presence would be welcome?"

"Oh." Sophie breathed out the word. "I cannot refuse your generous offer. I have been sharing the care for my grandmother with Mary, but to have someone else, if indeed your nurse should wish it..." She turned a questioning glance to him.

He liked the way her face grew animated when she was taken up with an idea. How could he have thought her expression veiled the first time they met?

"She should indeed," he assured her. "And when your grandmother grows better, I hope you will allow Jeannot to care for her more fully so you might attend some of the soirées in Paris?"

"If she *does* get better," Sophie said, worry evident in her tone.

"She will." Basile held her stare, as though it were

possible to chase away the doubts and fears by doing so. Zoé had been right. It was hard enough when a loved one was ill, but how much more difficult when one was on foreign soil!

They faced one another—she, seemingly lost in her thoughts, and he, content to look at her. The nearness of their pose, the awareness of it, finally shook him from his strange reluctance to leave.

"I will be off then," he said, lifting his hat and sweeping her a bow, his smile back in place.

She curtsied. "It was so good of you to call."

"I do not wish to interrupt your time outdoors. I shall see myself out." His eyes lingered as she brought the lavender stem up to her nose.

"Very well," she said.

As he moved toward the door, he resisted the urge to turn around and wondered if she followed him with her eyes when he departed. He could smell lavender long after he left the house.

CHAPTER 6

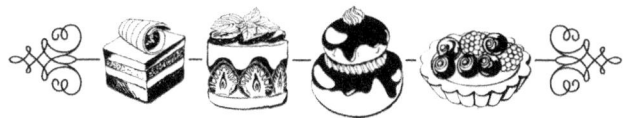

Sophie sat back down on the cold stone bench and watched Basile pull open the back door of the house and disappear into the dark corridor. She had to admit there was more to the gentleman than just play, for he had certainly shown himself a faithful friend. He sent a doctor—and no ordinary doctor! One who had waited upon the king himself. Not only that, but Basile had paid the man's bill so she would not be required to beg her ill grandmother for the sum. And then he had come to visit her...

Although she was not precisely sure why he had. He'd hardly stayed at all, and he had leapt at once to his feet as though he did not wish to be by her side a minute longer. He was a most puzzling gentleman. But, after all, a *kind*, puzzling gentleman.

She inhaled the clean lavender scent of the stalk that had been thin enough to tug free. Perhaps she should bring a few in to her grandmother's room to lighten the air. They were in full bloom and smelled heavenly.

Rather than go in search of a knife, she yanked at

another, thicker stalk, attempting to use her fingernail to snap it in two, but it was a fruitless endeavor. A knife it would have to be.

She turned as the door to the house opened again, and this time Sheldon appeared in the yard. She set her lips in a firm line, not pleased at his appearance but having little power to do anything about it. His presence would be harder to bear after the marquis's agreeable visit.

She lifted a hand as she walked toward him. "Good day, Sheldon. I am going inside to get a knife so I might cut some lavender for my grandmother."

He pivoted to walk with her. "I will accompany you, then."

To her surprise, he did so in silence as she requested a knife from Mary, then returned with her outdoors. It was unlike him to be so discreet. Perhaps he was chastened because today was the first day she had permitted Mary to allow him entrance since his bumbling proposal. However, she would not be the one to begin the conversation.

It was only when he'd sat on the bench and she began to cut the lavender that he spoke. "Sophie, I've been thinking. And I suppose I must offer you an apology for hinting that I would not see to my obligation of bringing you and your grandmother safely home."

Sophie looked up at him in surprise and saw an earnest expression on his face. Never before had she been so in charity with him. She went over to the bench and held out her hand. "'Tis very kind of you to offer the apology."

He pressed her hand, his cheeks growing flushed. "Well, I own it was not a gentlemanly thing to say. I have also arranged for a mantua-maker recommended by Mrs. Pertrand, who is attached to the embassy, although you will not have met her yet. Madame Meriaux will come tomorrow to take your measurements so you might walk out more soberly attired as befits the public mourning of Louis XV."

Sophie was not sure she liked being handled in such a way. It was as though he thought they were, in truth, betrothed. She hoped her grandmother would be able to meet the expenses of the gowns. Dropping her eyes, she managed a "thank you."

"How is your grandmother?" he asked, turning the subject before the moment could become uncomfortable.

She went back to cutting lavender, dropping the stalks in the shallow woven basket she had brought for the purpose. "Much the same, I am afraid. She spends most of her time resting, and any time she attempts to speak, it provokes a fit of coughing that leaves her quite exhausted."

Sheldon narrowed his eyes. "You are looking a little worn yourself. You must give the care of your grandmother entirely over to Mary. It would not do for you to grow ill."

She cocked her head with a look of exasperation. "I cannot leave my grandmother alone for such a trifling fear as that. And Mary certainly cannot manage all the care for her while still seeing that we have food to eat and clean rooms besides."

Turning her eyes back to her basket, she added, "But you may set your fears to rest on that head. The Marquis de Verdelle has promised to send over his old nurse, who is looking for something to do. He assured me of her willingness to assist us with the task of caring for my grandmother. It was most kind of him."

It was embarrassing to speak of the marquis as though they were truly familiar, but it was the one sure way to remind Sheldon she was not completely at his mercy.

Sure enough, he folded his arms over his ample chest,

although the tightness of his coat made the endeavor a difficult one. "I do not like your relationship with this man. I must tell you my feelings on the matter and will not be still."

Sophie assessed the lavender nestled on the straw weave, wondering if she had cut enough. It was probably sufficient. This thought pulled at her attention while she considered how best to answer.

"I thank you for your thoughts, but I shall be guided by my own. Basile is an old friend, and he means me no harm." It surprised her how easily the lie about their acquaintance slipped out, for she was in general a truthful person. But then he was easily coming to feel like a friend in their short, strange acquaintance.

"Well, as I have said before, you have a natural *naïveté* as a young, unmarried woman," Sheldon replied. "You cannot see the dangers he poses as clearly as I do."

"Shall we return indoors?" Sophie asked brightly. "I wish to bring these to my grandmother. I feel sure they will do her good."

Sheldon stood and tugged at his coat to right it. "Well, I suppose we can continue this discussion at another time." It came out in a petulant tone.

"Perhaps."

He turned to look at the garden. "You are most fortunate in having this outdoor space. I should have liked to have had it, but when my man of business learned of the two available properties for rent, he recommended I take the other one, for it is much larger. And indeed it is. It would take four of your sitting rooms to fill my drawing room."

"Yes, you chose well. As for me, I am partial to our modest rooms and the garden that comes behind them. I would much rather have that than a large drawing room." Sophie stepped back, allowing him to open the door to the house. "And although I have said it before, please allow me to thank you for your kindness in arranging all the details of our travel."

"Well." Sheldon frowned and looked down at his buckled shoes. "It was only natural if we are to be betrothed."

Sophie froze in place and opened her eyes at him. Did he truly think it? *Still?* How many ways did she have to make it clear to him?

"But you understand this is not to be the case, do you not? I believed your accompaniment was done out of kindness for our family and the friendship you once had with my father, not for any unspoken promise."

"We shall see. There is no need to discuss it now," Sheldon replied vaguely.

Any kindness Sophie had felt for him earlier dissipated like mist. "You must please excuse me. I wish to bring these to my grandmother, and I should not like for you to fall ill by spending too much time in a household where there is sickness."

"By George, you're right!" he exclaimed. He made a hurried bow. "I shall bid you good day, Sophie."

He left, and she let out a quiet huff of exasperation as she turned into the suite of bedrooms. There, she paused at the threshold and took in her normally vibrant grandmother lying in the bed, eyes shut. She brought the basket over to the dressing table and set it down before going over to pull the covers more comfortably around her grandmother.

"Sophie."

"Yes, Grandmama?" She paused in her movements and

sat on the side of the bed, taking her grandmother's hand in hers.

"Sheldon was here. I believe it is time to think about marrying him. I want to see you taken care of."

The words were spoken weakly and were accompanied by a fit of coughing that left Sophie uneasy but gave her the time she needed to consider how to respond.

"I wish you will not talk as though you are not going to make a full recovery, Grandmama. Do you know that the Marquis de Verdelle has promised to send his very own nurse to tend to you? Her name is Jeannot, and he assures me that you will soon recover under her ministrations."

When her grandmother offered no response, Sophie could not resist filling in the silence. "I promise you, all will be well. There is nothing to worry about. I have everything in hand here." She pasted a smile on her face, although her grandmother's eyes were closed, willing the smile to sound in her voice. It did not remove the worry from her grandmother's tone when she spoke again.

"You cannot be left to the mercy of this world with no fortune to save you." There was a long pause before she continued in the same feeble voice, interspersed with more bouts of coughing. "When this Jeannot person arrives, I want you to go out. Sheldon can get invitations. Until we can get you some black clothes, choose the more sober colors when in society. And do try to give Sheldon a chance."

It was the most her grandmother had spoken since she became ill, and Sophie was beginning to fear that anxious worry would hinder her grandmother from getting well. Nothing would keep Sophie from promising her whatever she desired.

She patted her hand. "Very well, Grandmama. I will do as you say."

THE DRESSMAKER ARRIVED first thing the next morning and took Sophie's measurements in a practiced manner as her assistant noted the figures. Madame Meriaux brought samples of what she said were being worn by everyone of note. She was quick to inform Sophie that the *monsieur* had ordered her to make up three gowns from any of these fabrics. Sophie offered her a tight-lipped smile, tempted to order only one just to prove to Sheldon that she made her own decisions. However, the truth was that she would need at least three gowns, if not more. In the end, she ordered three gowns made up of varying tones of gray and black that would be distinguished by touches of white or black embellishments. These gowns were promised in a week, with one fitting midway through.

No sooner had the mantua-maker left than another knock on the door brought Sheldon into their sitting room where Sophie was picking at the stitches of a flamboyant trim to an otherwise sober-colored gown. She stood.

"Sheldon, I am sorry but I do not have the time to visit just now. We are expecting the nurse to come for my grandmother, and I want to be ready for her."

"I will not stay," he assured her, then proceeded to belie these words by sitting without waiting to be invited. "I merely came to ensure that the dressmaker has shown you the samples and that you've had those gowns made up for you as I indicated."

Sophie breathed in through her nose as she smoothed

the carmine-colored ribbon she had already pulled free from the skirt. "It was kind of you to send the dressmaker, but quite unnecessary. I would have done so as soon as I had the chance."

"Yes, but in arranging it, I was able to have the bills sent directly to me rather than have them go through your grandmother, who is ill." He swiveled on his chair and looked behind him. "Perhaps Mary might bring us some tea."

"Sheldon." She stared at him in shock. "You should not be paying my dressmaker's bills, even temporarily. It is most improper."

He brought his attention back to her in surprise. "My dear, I am paying *all* of your bills. I thought you knew that. Your grandmother would not have been able to afford this trip or those gowns she commissioned for both of you before we left England had it not been for me."

Sophie felt the blood drain from her face and managed to choke out the words, "I did not know it." How in the world was she to pay him back? She would certainly need to if he were to be convinced they had no future.

He crossed one leg over the other. "Well, now you do. And you see why I had assumed an engagement between us was imminent."

She could only stare back at him mutely. How could her grandmother do this to her? Sophie had known how badly her grandmother wished to visit Paris, but to allow herself to be beholden to Sheldon Cholmsley like this? And she could not even discuss the matter with her grandmother now when she was so very ill.

"I was not privy to the information and would have objected most adamantly had I known," she said at last. "I will return the gowns." She would just have to wear those already in her possession.

"You cannot. Such a thing is not done, and you do need the mourning attire to be presentable in society. Mrs. Pertrand told me as much." He looked at her carefully. "You must not worry. We need not discuss the engagement at present. There will be time for that."

Any arguments she put forth now would only be wasted breath. Sophie did not know how she managed to continue a conversation when she was in such a state of upset. She managed to rid the house of its unwelcome visitor minutes before Basile's nurse arrived by claiming she had several items that needed mending. He seized on that disclosure by reminding her that she would have nothing so taxing to do as mending when she was married to him. It took everything in her not to whip the cocked hat out of Mary's hands and throw it at his head.

Madame Jeannot proved to be a gentle, reassuring presence. She spoke no English, but that did not stop her from endearing herself to Mary. Using gestures, she showed that she considered Mary to have authority over how the kitchen was run and would put all of her own efforts into tending to Mrs. Twisden. Sophie was exceedingly grateful to have her, for they *could* communicate, and she quite trusted the homemade remedies Jeannot had brought to alleviate her grandmother's suffering.

The nurse began by replacing her grandmother's pillow with one she had brought from the marquis's house, stuffed fat with goose down. She gently lifted Mrs. Twisden from behind and placed the more comfortable pillow underneath her head which eased her breathing. She approved of the lavender that Sophie had collected and even displayed a salve that contained some of it. This, she rubbed on Mrs. Twisden's chest and back that caused a hacking cough, but which seemed to allow her to sleep more peacefully.

After only a half day with Jeannot in the household, Sophie was inspired to take both of the nurse's hands in her own with a warm look of gratitude. "*Merci!*"

Jeannot brushed it off with a laugh and urged Sophie to go for a walk, which she decided to heed and called for Mary to accompany her.

Outside in the bright light that reflected off the beige stones of the buildings, they walked over to the short wall near the Seine and stood watching the river flow by. The sun had long since reached its zenith and was streaming through the streets on the opposite side of the river. Its rays danced on the ripples of water as a breeze lifted Sophie's curls. Her gaze focused dreamily on the boats that drifted by on the river's current. Some held bales of hay and others, produce. On others were the rustling of livestock. She turned to face right and spotted the tall spires of the great Notre Dame cathedral behind some of the buildings on the Île de la Cité.

A touch on her elbow yanked her out of her reverie and caused her to spin in alarm. Instead of finding some impertinent stranger who had dared to accost her, she came face to face with those compelling eyes of Basile Gervain.

"Mademoiselle Sophie," he said, smiling, as he bowed before her. "It is good to see you out of doors."

She recovered her composure and was able to smile in return. "Well, it is only because you had the goodness to send your nurse, who in two hours has already become indispensable to us."

She was learning to guard her heart whenever she was in Basile's presence. He was much too handsome and entirely out of her sphere. She well knew the danger of falling for him. But resisting him was hard when they met unexpectedly, and he looked at her as though he *cared* about her.

He held out an arm in invitation to slip hers into it, and they began to walk in the direction of Notre Dame. "Jeannot is *un trésor*, is she not?"

"The very best treasure," she replied with sincerity.

They walked quietly for a space, with the clip-clop of horses' hooves to their right, and the cries from sailors below as they greeted each other on the water or maneuvered to avoid collision. Mary walked several paces behind them.

Sophie turned to him suddenly. "It just occurred to me how odd it is we should meet by chance this way. Paris is not a small city."

She could see his eyes crinkle from her vantage point. "The city is much more intimate than you imagine, Sophie. One is forever bumping into friends here—and, *hélas*, into those one would rather not meet."

She digested this as he added, "But I live just there on that street." He pointed ahead to the next side street that cut across to the Seine. "So you see, I am not so very far from you."

"How fortunate," she replied lightly, then could think of nothing further to add. She found herself oddly tongue-tied. This was not like her and she wondered if it had anything to do with all the time she had spent indoors with her grandmother. It must have dulled her wits.

"Has Mr. Cholmsley been providing you the comfort of a fellow countryman? He lives next door to you, I remember, for I had an invitation sent there from Madame Dubigny."

"He does indeed live next door." Sophie twisted her lips wryly, thinking with plunging insides of their recent conversation. "Though I cannot say he brings me much comfort. He would like to marry me despite my repeated assurances that we should not suit."

"I hope he has not been pressing his advantage unfairly while your grandmother is unwell." Basile slowed his steps when she did not answer him right away.

She darted a glance at him and chose full honesty. How she needed a friend. "He is pressing his advantage, but I fear that he has had cause to do so."

"Ah. So your affections *are* engaged," he replied after a slight pause, his voice hard.

"No," she replied with a bitter laugh. "They are most certainly not and are not likely to be. But I discovered that, unbeknownst to me, my grandmother has allowed Sheldon to pay not only for our stay in Paris but even such things as the bills incurred at the mantua-maker's." She looked at him, willing him to understand. "It is intolerable. Of course he will expect something in return. And now I cannot even task my grandmother with it. She is too unwell."

Basile was silent as they walked, and she began to fear he was disgusted by her. To be so impoverished. To be something of a kept woman, although it was through no choice of her own.

"It seems there is only one thing to it. You will have to fall head over heels in love with an eligible man—and quickly."

She met this sally with a feeble grin. "Oh, why certainly. Such a thing may be had at the snap of one's fingers."

"In all seriousness," he went on. "He cannot pressure you into a union you do not wish for."

"He is confident that I do not know what I want and

that I will come to discover it when he has presented his case for marriage in several different ways." She allowed her voice to drip with irony to relieve some of her annoyance.

"I know men like that," Basile said. "They are seldom convinced they might be wrong. They are never a pleasure to be around." Sophie laughed, and he paused, pulling her to a stop. "I have not asked you where you wished to go."

"I was merely taking air. But I suppose I should turn back toward my home." She gave him a look. "Even though I do trust Jeannot entirely."

Basile directed his steps down the street where he'd said he lived. They would be walking a full square to bring her back to her house.

"When will you do more than just take air?" he asked her. "Have you plans to reenter the social scene again? I am sure it is what your grandmother would wish."

"Odd you should say that," she replied. "It *is* what my grandmother wishes. She told me so, but with her in a state of such weakness I fear to heed her."

"In that case, I will have an invitation sent for Madame Beauchamp's dinner tomorrow night. And really, I think you will be pleasing your grandmother by attending. I can have Zoé's mother include you in their party so that you will be accompanied."

"It is kind of you," Sophie said slowly. "I would like it, if it should not trouble Madame Sainte-Croix. I...am not sure it is the right thing to do, despite my grandmother telling me to go. What if something should happen to her whilst I am out on a pleasure jaunt?"

"You will ask Jeannot to tell you if she has any fears that your grandmother might take a turn for the worse. She has skill with healing, and I think she will know if there is cause for concern." Basile pointed on the opposite side of the street a little farther ahead. "That is my house."

It was a grand structure whose façade took up a good portion of the street. The building was made of limestone and there was an iron gate in its center. As they drew abreast, she looked through the opening where she was afforded a view of the courtyard and garden. The house was a pleasing, welcoming edifice. Grand and yet built in simple lines with elegant paned windows set in even rows.

"Beautiful." She turned to look at him. "Your family has owned it for generations, I imagine?"

He nodded, and she bit her lip as a thought occurred. What had they in common? Why, nothing. She had to ask him—had to know. When she brought her eyes to rest on his handsome bearing, he was looking at her curiously.

"Why in *heaven's* name are you acting the friend to me when I am so clearly beneath you in station? Your family, your title…everything is centuries old. Does it not turn your head at times?" She laughed, attempting to cover up the embarrassment over her impetuous but honest words.

He continued to study her, and it only made her face grow warm until she needed to turn forward again to escape his gaze.

"I am accustomed to my station, so I suppose I don't heed it," he answered at last. "I'm not grateful for it—not as I should be. I am more grateful for my family seat in the Champagne region. In truth, I am the last of four brothers and it is only the fickle hand of Fate that chose me as marquis."

His lips tightened, and he moved on without saying more, leading her to the end of the street and turning right to bring her back to the humbler lodgings that were temporarily her own. So, he had not wished to inherit his title then. This was news to her. Despite her sympathy for his position, it had also not escaped her notice that he had not answered her question.

They spoke only of benign observations as they walked and she considered the moment for honesty to have passed. However, when they reached the front of her house, he stopped and faced her.

"As for your first question." He leaned in until she was pinned underneath his very direct regard. "I befriended you initially on a whim to enliven my stay here while I am forced to be in Paris. But you must not think I regret the acquaintance, for I do not. You do not bore me."

"Heavens," she said, in possession of herself again at this sobering reminder. "You overwhelm me with your compliments, sir."

He laughed. "You think it poor praise, Sophie, but believe me when I say there are few people indeed of whom I can say the same."

Sophie acknowledged this with a nod, for what could she say in return? It was clear he had not lost his heart to her, and she would do well not to be a fool and lose hers to him.

CHAPTER 7

Basile left Sophie at her door, conscious of his clumsy attempt to add distance to their relationship by speaking of whims—and conscious also of the inexplicable regret that came when he walked on alone. All rational thought dictated he keep her at arm's length, thus shielding her from false promises. Yet, the irrational beat of his heart did not care to create distance, not when the unexpected glimpse of her staring out over the city of Paris caused his feet to stop dead in their tracks. The sight had naturally led him to offer her his arm so she might stroll with him, and that had brought him as much pleasure as he could hope for. He could think of far worse fates.

He would not go home just yet. Not before he had sorted through the puzzling feelings that surfaced whenever he was around Sophie. He headed back toward the Seine and retraced the same steps, this time continuing on to the small island from which sprang the Notre Dame. His thoughts were elusive, and he did not attempt to tame them until he came to stand in front of the centuries-old edifice. There, he lifted his eyes to the slim vertical arches that rose up to the heavens, with the three portals carved with Biblical figures that included the last judgment. Above the central portal was a magnificent rose window that could only be described as a wonder considering when it had been built.

When she had asked why he had befriended her, he'd played the impulse off as a means to pass the time and evade boredom. The words had been almost cruel, though he'd had no intention to wound. He had left her in no doubt of his determination not to seek a relationship of a more serious nature. It was the proper, rational thing to do. And yet, was he being truthful with himself? It had indeed started as a game to pass the time, but her worry over her grandmother slipped past his defenses, and her dependence on the Englishman galled. Her well-being mattered to him as though she had indeed been a friend of long date.

He turned from the great cathedral and headed toward the English embassy on rue Jacob, where he knew Zoé would be. Charles Arlington had sent a few of the French families an invitation to drink tea, and as the ambassador was well-liked among the French, it had naturally been accepted. Basile had also received an invitation, although the gathering was not supposed to be a large one. It was more likely due to his friendship with Zoé than his title.

When he arrived, he found the drawing room packed with both English and French. Lord Stormont, the English ambassador, stood in conversation with M. and Madame Necker, and Basile went over to greet him before turning to look over the crowd. Zoé was standing beside Charles, and upon catching sight of him, she lifted her hand and waved him over.

"Good day, Charles. Zoé," he added, making her a

magnificent leg, which she tutted away without bothering to curtsy.

"Never mind that. Charles has informed me that *Le Ranelagh* will open at last on Monday, and he is invited to attend the opening ball. *Enfin*—rather it was Lord Stormont who was invited, but he was given extra tickets." She paused for breath, adding, "You must come with me, of course. It is the highest honor to be seen there."

Basile glanced at Charles, whose friendly greeting was dimmed by what he suspected was jealousy. Zoé was not going about her pursuit in the right way, but he was not going to refuse her proposal when it suited his own desires.

"I shall be delighted, but I won't need one of your tickets. I have been offered an annual subscription and agreed to it, although I must be out of my mind. I do not plan to stay in Paris for as long." He turned to address Charles. "Who is to be of the party?"

Zoé did not allow Charles to answer. "You have an annual subscription and did not think to tell me?"

He shrugged. "I did not think it worthy news."

"Well," she exclaimed, her blue eyes sparkling with pleasure. "It matters not that you will return to Verdelle, for you may continue to provide me with tickets even after you leave."

Charles's expression lightened and he offered Basile a smile. "To answer your question, we have not got up a party yet. The embassy was given ten tickets, and Mademoiselle Sainte-Croix and her parents and sister will use four of them. Lord Stormont and myself will take another two. If you will not need any, we will find a ready use for the other four tickets."

"I will not. Charles, will you excuse me if I speak with Zoé for a moment in private?" Basile asked. Charles's expression grew closed again, but he nodded and stepped aside.

"What is it?" Zoé asked, full of curiosity when they were alone.

"I want you to accompany Sophie to Madame Beauchamp's party tomorrow night. Will you do it?"

Zoé gave a pleased gasp. "Is her grandmother well then? I am so glad to hear it."

"No, she is still unwell, but I have sent my old nurse to help care for her, and I think it would do Sophie good to escape from her worries for a while." He was conscious of Zoé's careful scrutiny, which he did not like and did his best to weather.

"Hm." After a moment's speculation, she promised that she would visit Sophie to offer escort and be sure she would be free to come. "And you will wish to invite her to the Ranelagh ball, of course," she added. "I am sure she will not have seen anything like it. The decorations are said to be most extraordinary, and the ball is held outdoors."

It had already occurred to Basile to invite Sophie to it, but he did not wish to be too eager. "We shall see. In the meantime, I thank you for your services in bringing Sophie tomorrow night."

BASILE WAS UNCHARACTERISTICALLY early to Madame Beauchamp's party, and it was already crowded before Sophie arrived. When Basile at last caught her shy smile across a packed room, he went very still and found that his breath did not come as easily as it usually did. The sensation was so foreign it kept him rooted in place. *There is*

something there, he thought. *This is no ordinary acquaintance I shall soon forget.*

She was standing at Zoé's side, and her hair powdered close to her natural color set her apart from the crowd. She wore a dark plum gown not unlike the blacks that the rest of the noble and genteel society were wearing. Her face had little of the powder and rouge that fashionable women wore, but it suited her. Her eyes had enough expression to equal the most vivid of colors. Still, he was curious to see what she would look like were she to dress in more of a French fashion with white-powdered hair, carefully placed patches on her cheek, and a gown in a more daring cut.

M. Cholmsley peeled himself away from a small circle and went over to her. His proprietary air was unmistakable, and Basile stepped forward to do something about it. He then came to an abrupt halt, realizing that Claudia Bordenave would spot him if he went in that direction. She had appeared at the last two evening soirées he had attended, and he began to think that someone was apprising her of his schedule. He could not seem to escape her no matter how hard he tried. She lost no opportunity to bring up their past engagement and list the reasons why they would still suit. It was extremely wearisome, and he had begun to feel hounded. Perhaps he could escape her this evening.

For some reason, her regard had settled on Sophie and the peacock and remained fixed there. She had always been a cunning woman, and he feared she had connected Sophie to himself and was looking to make trouble. Thankfully, Claudia moved away minutes later just as Zoé pulled Sophie from Mr. Cholmsley and engaged her in conversation he could have no part of since it was in French.

That was Basile's cue. He approached Sophie at the moment Charles appeared at Zoé's side. Once Charles had greeted Zoé, he had no eyes for anyone else, which left Basile and Sophie to a blessedly uninterrupted conversation.

"*Enchanté, ma* Sophie," he said, bending down to kiss her proffered hand. "You have arrived."

"*Your* Sophie?" she repeated, blushing even as she smiled. However, she said nothing further regarding his endearment. "Thank you again for sending your dear nurse to help us. I would not have dared to leave my grandmother had I not had someone as competent as Jeannot to see to her needs. She has even managed to win Mary over, and they find ways to communicate without a shared language."

"Jeannot needed no persuading to come, I assure you. She has been pestering me about providing her with an heir to dote upon, and without that, she must have something else to do."

Sophie had no chance to respond, which was just as well since he had been speaking of heirs and himself in the same breath. Grégoire passed by them on his circuit of the room and made her an elegant bow. "Mademoiselle Twisden, I am delighted to see you are out in company again. Your grandmother, I trust, is much improved?"

"She is...better, but I fear it will be some time before she can rejoin society. I hope she may not spend her entire visit in Paris tied to her bed. She was so looking forward to seeing her friends again."

"One must hope, indeed," Grégoire said.

A movement in their direction caught Basile's eye, and he groaned inwardly. La Bordenave had spotted him after all and as she approached, Cholmsley eyed her progress, glancing between the widow and Sophie. Basile quietly ground his teeth. Would he never be free of that woman?

And must Sophie forever put up with that overbearing coxcomb? No! Something must be done.

"*Bonsoir*, Basile."

As Claudia curtsied, the wide skirts of her gown forced Sophie to step backwards. His mind calculating rapidly, he bit back a protest to see her treated that way when she was the superior of the two women. Sophie's affronted look went as quickly as it came, and she schooled her features. She did not so much as look at Basile, and it seemed to him as though she accepted the indignity. It was time to put an end to La Bordenave's pretensions.

"Good evening, Madame Bordenave. What a most propitious meeting, for I am able to introduce you to my *fiancée*, Mademoiselle Sophie Twisden."

Taking full advantage of Claudia's shocked attention fixed on him, he caught Sophie's eyes and tried to read her reaction to his impetuous announcement. He allowed his face to reveal nothing, but his eyes compelled her to accept his falsehood. In that moment, the only thing that mattered was that he could be free of Claudia's constant presence and Sophie might dispense with her unpleasant suitor. He would worry about the rest later.

Sophie's color heightened, but her face did not express any more of what she was feeling than his. She held his gaze, seeming to weigh the meaning of his false proposal. Somehow he knew, dangerous though it was, that she would not hold him to it. It was a dastardly thing to do, he knew, but he trusted her to understand why he had done it. He made a vow to himself that she would not suffer from it.

"Is that so?" Claudia's voice hardened as she turned to stare at Sophie.

Sophie pulled her eyes from Basile and turned up the corners of her lips.

"Yes, Basile and I are betrothed, although it has not been publicly announced before now. I had thought we decided to wait until Grandmama was better before announcing it, did we not, *chéri*?" She looked at him sweetly and he could hear the faintest edge to her voice. It was only because he was coming to know her that he could hear it at all.

Basile knew what was required of him, and he brushed past Claudia and held Sophie's hand, bringing it to his lips.

"Forgive me, *mon amour*. In my ardor, I was too eager to share our good news with the world. But, of course, I should have waited until your grandmother was well enough."

"Betrothed! You and Miss Twisden?" Claudia exclaimed in a ringing voice as her incredulous stare rolled from Sophie to him. Basile could not understand why she'd spoken in English until several of the party turned her way, including the bug-eyed stare of Mr. Cholmsley. The room began to hum as the women whipped open their fans to spread the news.

"Sophie," Mr. Cholmsley thundered, moving toward her at once. "What is this woman saying? You must correct her."

Sophie looked up at her compatriot with a smile that could not have been more convincing. "Please wish us happy, Sheldon. The marquis and I have reached an agreement."

Mr. Cholmsley seemed lost for words, but he stood in front of her and begged that she explain herself, which she did in a low voice that Basile had trouble catching over the hum of the masses. His every attention was on her.

"Sheldon, leave it, I beg of you," she said. "I have

already told you there is no hope for a match between us. And now you will understand why."

Claudia, not wishing to have her message lost for the remaining crowd, added in French for good measure, "I declare, I almost thought you would never marry, Basile. I suppose the need for an heir must cause one to make hasty steps in that direction."

She spotted Armand advancing, his eyes on Basile, and pounced. "Monsieur de Galladier, you are a most intimate friend of the marquis. You must tell me all about their *coup de foudre*!"

She took his arm and whisked him away but not before Basile heard Armand say, "Madame, you have guessed the matter. It was indeed love at first sight."

Basile sent a questioning glance at Grégoire, who answered. "You may be sure he will know how to handle her." He leaned in to murmur the rest. "He is only naïve when it comes to his own affections. He knows who La Bordenave is."

Grégoire glanced at Sophie, who seemed to look anywhere but at them, then dipped his chin to Basile to murmur, "I shall leave you to your oh-so-*charmante fiancée*."

Amidst the whispers, Basile tucked Sophie's hand into his arm, and she walked at his side with her head held high. He led her through the open doors of the terrace to the stone balustrade that looked over the garden at the back of the house. Now outdoors, he gulped at the fresh air. There were steps that led down to the garden, which had couples taking a turn in the rectangular stretch of grass. Other couples sat more discreetly on the stone benches in verdant arches.

"You must think I have gone mad," he began. The night

air was cool and perfumed with flowers and freshly cut grass. "Allow me to explain—"

"It is possible I have already guessed all." Sophie breathed in and lifted her gaze to the sky, which was particularly clear and showed a host of stars across its expanse. "I understand that this is not a true betrothal, but that you did it for your own purposes—and perhaps for me in that way you have of playing harmless games."

Basile could not answer this. It certainly did not put him in the best light, but he did not deserve better.

They walked on, crossing underneath one of the arched trellises that had fragrant blooming roses intertwined from one side to the other. "In all honesty, you have saved me from the most unwelcome attentions of Sheldon Cholmsley. And I can only suspect that your motives in proposing were for similar reasons."

"It is just so," Basile replied, glancing at her from the side and trying to read her expression. He could only make out her profile lightly in the moonlight, but he could detect her scent and admired the soft skin of her hand when he placed his over it. Walking next to her brought him pleasure, despite his unease over his impulsive announcement. "Now that I have given my word, however, I engage to honor my commitment."

"No, no." Sophie pulled him to a stop, and he could barely discern the furrow in her brow. "I shall not hold you to it. I understood the spontaneous manner in which you announced it. I have no wish to force you to honor a commitment you made under such circumstances. I assure you, I did not look for your proposal."

Basile smiled to himself, prey to relief that she would free him of his engagement so rashly given and piqued despite himself that she was so adamant in rejecting his offer. He allowed silence to reign again as he considered his words. It was a bit late for that, but he would move more cautiously.

"Well, I shall not force you into a marriage that was not of your choosing, simply by having announced the match publicly. But here is what I think on the matter. Before you return to London, you might choose to announce that you have come to the realization you prefer to unite yourself with a man from your own country. Hopefully after M. Cholmsley has either left or set his attention on someone else." He smiled at her and gave a light tug on her arm. "You are therefore obliged to regretfully withdraw your promise. I engage to be suitably devastated but declare myself perfectly in line with your reasons. Nothing shall impinge upon your honor."

From what he could glimpse of her expression in the dark, Sophie did not look entirely convinced at the ease of his proposed rupture. But when she turned to him, her tone betrayed no hesitation. "I think that will answer very well. And in the meantime, I may enjoy my stay in Paris without being persecuted by proprietary men."

"And I by such women," Basile added. He exhaled and flashed her a smile born of relief. Sophie had not demurred over his crazy scheme, and perhaps he would indeed be free of Claudia. By the time he and Sophie ended the charade, he would be safely back on his estate beyond the widow's reach. His relief made him want to offer something to Sophie—an unaccustomed personal disclosure.

"I should probably explain that I was once betrothed to Claudia, and she broke off the engagement for a man with better prospects. Ever since she arrived in Paris in her widowed state, she has not stopped hounding me with proof of all the reasons we should make a match of it again.

I, of course, have learned my lesson and cannot be tempted."

"So you do understand to some degree what I am facing with Sheldon," she said.

"All too well." He pressed the hand that rested on his arm. "I promise you, this will be an advantageous move for us both."

The garden began to fill with more of the guests with people coming nearer—ostensibly with the object to listen. It would not do to discuss details here with such a public audience, and he must certainly call on her tomorrow to align their stories. He glanced up into the vast, candlelit drawing room, beckoning in its gaiety. At the door stood one of the king's courtiers, and he made a signal to Basile that he wished to speak to him.

Ah. Basile had not yet been summoned to Versailles, but it appeared the time to show his allegiance to Louis XVI was now upon him. He only wondered how quickly he would have to obey the summons.

"Shall we go inside?"

CHAPTER 8

Sophie's *tête-à-tête* lasted only a short time before Basile brought her back indoors. Within minutes of stepping inside, they were drawn from one conversation to another with people she scarcely knew but who were all brimming with curiosity. She was hard-pressed to hide her alarm, even with Basile at her side. It was more from fear of questions she would have trouble answering than his sudden declaration, although to find oneself suddenly engaged without a prior understanding did pose an upset to one's equilibrium.

She had pretended a very natural indifference to his announcement and assured him that by no means would she hold him to it. This, indeed, was true. The thought of trapping a man into marriage was abhorrent to her, even if he had created the trap and stumbled into it all on his own. She would never force his hand.

But to be the object of such scrutiny was unnerving. Zoé was the first to come over to them the minute she and Basile stepped indoors.

"How very, very naughty of you to become secretly

engaged and not tell even me, Basile." Zoé managed a pout which soon split into a grin. "But I am so happy for you both. In sooth, I had guessed your feelings ran deep when you asked me to escort Sophie here tonight."

Before Sophie could recover from *that* disclosure, Zoé slipped her arm through Sophie's and led her away, saying over her shoulder, "I shall learn all the news from her, for I know you will tell me nothing."

That caused Sophie's heart to accelerate, a feat she had thought not possible considering how nervous she was already. How could she prevaricate without any time to prepare, and to a woman who had shown herself to be a friend?

"So tell me everything," Zoé said, leading her over to a false column built into the wall and painted with ivy. "I want to know all the details of how you caught Basile when no other woman could do so."

"Oh, well...I suppose we..." Heat rushed up Sophie's face as she struggled to think how to answer. "We met in England first, you see. And I suppose it must have been love..." Her words trailed away when she saw Zoé's look of disbelief.

"That will not do, my dear," Zoé leaned in to whisper. "Basile has told me that he in fact met you here in Paris, and only a few days ago."

Sophie grew hot with embarrassment which caused a surge of irritation to rise. How dare he put her in such a position! "Then why do you pester me about a love story? You must know it is not true."

Zoé's changeable features moved to chagrin. "Oh, did I anger you? I am sorry. I thought it *might* be true. For you see, I am a romantic at heart, and I have never seen Basile act this way. I was quite convinced he did indeed fall for you at first sight."

Tumultuous thoughts and feelings raged inside of Sophie. One of his closest friends thought his attachment was real? What if it was? *No, no—it can't be! Don't travel that dangerous, futile path of thought.*

When Sophie did not respond, Zoé tugged at her arm, which she was still holding on to. "Oh, do forgive me for causing you distress. I can see that you do not like this subject at all."

Sophie attempted a smile that would not appear bitter. If it was this difficult to explain their sham betrothal to Zoé, who was something of a friend, then it would only be harder with everyone else.

"So you have not fallen in love," Zoé said quietly, underneath the murmur of voices that filtered around them as she studied Sophie's face. "It is a betrothal that is not meant to last?"

"'Tis only to keep persistent suitors from harassing me, and I believe Basile has the same objective." She lifted her gaze to meet Zoé's. "At least that is what he seemed to have in mind when he announced it."

Zoé's eyes opened very wide. "Do you mean you did not agree in advance to pretend a betrothal? Oh, that is *infâme*! And just like Basile to do it. That is why I was never tempted to make a push for him, myself. Not," she added dismissively, "that I've ever had the slightest *tendresse* for him."

Sophie thought she had no blushes left, but she was wrong. She had not intended to throw Basile to the wolves. "Will you kindly keep this to yourself and not tell Basile I have told you this, for I should not wish to embarrass him."

"Have no fear on that head." Zoé reached out for two

lemonades from a servant who was passing by. "Basile is never embarrassed, although he deserves to be."

She handed a drink to Sophie, whose tongue was cleaving to the roof of her mouth. The sweet lemonade was at first unpleasant, but the cold liquid soothed and calmed her as it went down.

"Nevertheless, I will keep this secret," Zoé said. "I may look frivolous, but I am a good friend to have. I do not gossip." She sipped her lemonade, her eyes drifting across the room to where the English ambassador stood.

Sophie followed her look and crossed that of Sheldon's. As soon as he caught sight of her, he marched forward to take her hostage with his speech. Zoé took one look at his face and said, "I believe he will have his say no matter what I do, but do not forget that you have promised to leave with me, so you must not give into his entreaties if he orders you to leave early." She moved from Sophie's side just as Sheldon arrived.

"Sophie, there you are. After that most shocking announcement, you disappeared before I had a chance to find out what this was all about. Where were you?"

"Kindly keep your voice down." Sophie attempted to soften her admonition with a smile. "Although we are surrounded by French speakers, many of them *do* speak English also and you are calling unwelcome attention to us."

"Very well. But you must answer my question. I did not even know you would be here tonight. Who is staying with your grandmother?"

"Jeannot, the former nurse to the m—" She stopped. "My *fiancé*'s former nurse. He has graciously lent her to bring my grandmother back to health."

Sheldon studied her with narrowed eyes before leaning

in. "This betrothal has come about too quickly. When did he request your hand in marriage? When had he the time to do so?"

Sophie thought quickly. "He came to visit me. He asked me in our garden, and I told him yes."

Sheldon's frown lines grew pronounced. "Does your grandmother know?"

She paused—*oh dear, what to tell Grandmama?*—then shook her head. "No, she does not."

At this, his look of tension eased. "You see, all this has been done without any guidance, and in a foreign country. You are under the spell of this land, for in England we do not go and betroth ourselves to someone we scarcely know without the guidance of those who know better. Your father entrusted your care to me."

When he saw her look, he added, "In so many words."

The number of people gathering near to listen had grown, and Sophie laid a hand on his arm. "It would be better if this conversation were had at another moment and in a more private setting."

Sheldon looked around as though seeing for the first time the faces alert for gossip. "You may be sure it will be," he seethed quietly. "I shall take it upon myself to visit you. Perhaps your grandmother will receive me."

That was the last thing Sophie wanted, and she replied firmly, "Perhaps. But not until she is well."

"Let us hope this news does not finish her," Sheldon said grimly, and since he gave no indication he would move from her side, she curtsied and turned to see if she might find a friendly face elsewhere in the crowd.

The rest of the evening was no easier. Basile came to apologize, saying that one of the courtiers had informed him he was summoned to Versailles immediately. He would return as soon as the king had given him leave to do so. With Zoé speaking with Mr. Arlington, Sophie felt like she had lost her last friend.

More people sought introductions, no matter how flimsy, so they might learn of her story with the marquis. She was assured just how sought-after he was and how astonishing a thing it was that a simple Englishwoman with very little fashion could catch his heart in such a way. This was said with a laugh, supposedly meant to take the sting out of the words, but which seemed to make them more poisonous. Sophie could only reply that it was indeed unaccountable and that there was no explaining the ways of the heart. She was more than ready to leave the soirée at two o'clock in the morning, when Zoé was at last ready to depart, urged on by Madame Sainte-Croix. She decided that if she was given a choice, it would be the last time she attended a party with Zoé, whose aim, it appeared, was to be the last one to leave.

AFTER RECEIVING the message that the king had asked for him and having bid farewell to Sophie, Basile returned home from the dinner to gather some things he would need for an extended stay at court. He dearly hoped the king would not keep him there overly long. Perhaps he could claim a betrothal as an excuse to get away. Then again...was it wise to announce a betrothal that would not be carried through?

He rubbed his chin as the carriage rattled over the packed dirt roads and headed out of the city. It was probably better not to bring up the betrothal on his own, although the queen would certainly hear of it at some point and wish for all the details. He did not know Marie-Antoinette well, but from what little he knew, she would likely expect a story embellished with every romantic detail.

Basile did not often question himself, but his impulse was proving difficult to reason away. It mattered little that Sophie would eventually leave France and that what he had said was true—it was possible to end a betrothal without either of them facing scandal. She would not be improved by his public declaration, and she would face the same worries at the end of it that she did now. His lips tightened into a thin line and he stretched out his legs, irritated with himself for being so hasty.

When Basile became marquis, he had chosen not to have a room in the palace, although it had been offered to him. He explained in the most diplomatic way at his disposal that he was not a member of the king's advisory circle and therefore would not wish to take up the space of someone who spent more time in Versailles than he. He was allowed to maintain his own small house nearby, and that was his destination when he finally arrived after three in the morning, pulling his sleepy servants out of bed to attend to him.

The next morning, he removed his sword before entering the king's chamber and appeared before the king, bowing very low. "*Majesté, votre serviteur.*"

"Marquis," the king replied, with a nod and gestured for him to sit at one of the velvet-covered chairs in the room before turning his attention back to the Duc de Lauzun.

Basile did as ordered, waving away a glass of Bordeaux, and struck up a conversation with the Comte d'Artois, who was also waiting on his brother the king's pleasure.

"I am to understand that the Château de la Muette will host an open ball beginning on Monday. Will you attend it?" Basile asked.

"Le Ranelagh?" The count drank of his wine. "It will depend on the king. He will not attend this early in the court's mourning period, but he may give me leave to do so. Do you have a subscription?"

"Yes, and I plan to attend if I have leave." Basile looked up as the queen swept into the king's cabinet, followed by her attendants. He leapt to his feet along with the other gentlemen.

The queen came first to the king and curtsied deeply as all conversation ceased. Then her eyes roved around the room until they landed on Basile, her eyes suddenly intent. A ping of warning settled in his breast. She knew.

"You may continue with your conversations," she announced. Turning to her husband, she added, "I only wished to hear from Monsieur le Marquis about his betrothal to the Englishwoman, Mademoiselle Twisden."

All eyes turned to Basile, causing his breath to seize. If he were the blushing sort...

He moved forward and made another elaborate leg to his queen. "Your Majesty is remarkably well connected, and I am so pleased to hear it. I hope I may have the favor of your approval."

She indicated for him to rise. "Why, certainly. How did you meet her? What is this romantic story? I must have it." The conversation did not quite resume, but the king had at least turned back to the duke on his right.

Basile did not take his eyes off Marie-Antoinette, but he felt the attention of everyone in the room waiting for his answer. What seemed an innocent invention hours before became twisted as he contemplated lying to his queen.

"I fear our story will disappoint you. We met briefly when I was touring England and Scotland before I came into the marquisate, but other than discovering a mutual delight in each other's company, we did not think to pursue a courtship." He licked his lips. "Imagine my surprise when I stumbled upon her outside of Stohrer!"

"And when was this?" she asked, her lovely eyes alight with interest. Basile could understand why men were so captivated by her, although he would never draw so near to a flame that could not but singe.

"Not much above a week ago," he admitted.

"*Voyons!*" she exclaimed. "It is a love match, then. *Un véritable coup de foudre* if you can betroth yourself so quickly. I am to understand that you have been an elusive heart to capture in Paris. It needed only this Englishwoman."

"I admit 'tis so, madame. If only you will countenance it, our joy will be complete." His thoughts ran quickly. He needed to prepare for the eventual rupture by sowing doubt. "Of course, we have some obstacles to overcome."

"Love removes all obstacles," the queen said as she smiled upon him. She then took leave of her king and swept out in much the same way she had come.

Her only purpose in entering the king's chamber, then, had been to hear his story. A slight apprehension that was much like nausea settled over him. He would have to make this betrothal convincing and make their rupture even more so.

CHAPTER 9

Sophie's grandmother seemed more at ease under Jeannot's skilled care, but Sophie did not dare upset her grandmother by asking about the bills Sheldon had accumulated for the gowns and all the rest. And she had no qualms about refusing to admit Sheldon to see Mrs. Twisden when he came the next day for his promised remonstrance.

"Surely, you have taken the time to think about what I said," he began, after giving her the briefest of bows and charging his way into the sitting room. "It is not too late to pull out of this betrothal. After all, this was not announced in London, and there will be no scandal attached to your name if you were to do so."

"I have no intention of pulling out of the engagement," she said firmly, gesturing for him to sit. He would want to have his say, and she might as well hear it now when there were no eager ears to listen.

Ignoring her invitation, he paced to the other side of the room, then turned to face her. "Have you told your grandmother yet?"

"I did not deem it wise this morning when I went in to see her. She is far from well."

"It is clear to me that the news will not be well received. You know it and I know it." He pinned her with his scrutiny. "Otherwise, you would have told her by now."

"Joyful news can cause an overset in a person's health nearly as much as sober news," Sophie replied calmly, although her thoughts raced from the precariousness of her situation. "I do not wish for her to have any excitement whatsoever."

"I believe I should see her myself." His face became mulish.

"That is quite out of the question. And she would not thank you for witnessing her in a state of illness, for you are not family"—Sophie's conscience struck her even amidst what was growing into a firm dislike of the man—"despite how well you have cared for us, and for that I do thank you."

"I do not see what I am to do here in Paris, now that you are betrothed to someone else," he grumbled. "She and I have points to discuss given these unpleasant developments in regards to our connection. I would leave at once, except that I have several engagements with people in the embassy and they would not like for me to cry off."

"You must do as you see fit," Sophie said, turning as Mary came into the room. She indicated for her to set the tea on the table, then sat and gestured once again for Sheldon to do the same. The maid finished setting everything out and left the room. After a glance at his face, Sophie softened and she poured him a cup of tea. From his point of view, her behavior must seem highly ungrateful. "I do hope you will accept my decision and that we can remain friends."

"*Hmph.*" He stared down at the fob attached to his waistcoat. "Your betrothal is of such a sudden nature, perhaps it will not last. I am a patient man."

Sophie gritted her teeth. "I certainly hope it will not keep you from looking around for a lady who will be honored to become your wife," she said, listening to the sounds of Jeannot and Mary conferring in the kitchen in two different languages.

He finished his cup in silence, then sighed. "I will have to talk to the marquess about your arrangements here in Paris. I am sure we can come to an agreement. It makes no sense that I should be made to settle the bills of a woman with whom I have no hope of sharing a future. It is only natural that he should wish to take them over."

Sophie felt her face blanch with understanding of the humiliation that awaited her. "You cannot...you cannot think to do that."

He looked at her in surprise. "Whyever not? *I* should not like to allow another man to be paying for the expenses of my betrothed. It is most inappropriate and sends the wrong message."

"But no one knows of your assistance to our family," she replied as a new fear assailed her. "I should hope you are not spreading it about at the embassy to whom we owe our sojourn in Paris."

Sheldon shifted. "Oh, as to that..."

His non-answer did nothing to relieve her fears. So, everyone at the embassy knew of her impoverished state. Mary reentered the room, this time bringing an apricot cake. She set it in front of Sophie, who cut a small slice for Sheldon, although he had a hearty appetite. It was petty, she knew, but tears of humiliation stung her eyes. Tears she would not let him see.

Composing herself, she handed him his plate and refilled his cup, then she sipped her own tea to gain fortitude. "I beg you will not discuss this matter with the marquis. Allow me the dignity of becoming his charge once the ceremony occurs."

He spooned a morsel of cake into his mouth, answering through his bites. "You know little of these affairs, Sophie. Trust me when I tell you it is much better this way, and the gentleman will certainly expect me to call upon him."

Although she had not had breakfast, Sophie could eat nothing. The horror of her situation had become all too clear. It was one thing for Basile to know that Sheldon was paying her bills. It was quite another for him to be handed the stack of them with the expectation that he would pay. Why, they were nothing to each other! They were even less than she and Sheldon.

When she thought about it though, she grudgingly realized that Sheldon did have somewhat of a point. And Basile was the one who had gotten her into this mess, hadn't he? He could surely afford its complications. She knew instinctively he would not hold the debt over her head the way Sheldon did—using it to try to manipulate her behavior. And oh, what it would be like to be free from Sheldon's financial hold over her!

But still, it was nothing short of humiliating, and she could only hope that Sheldon would think the better of it.

THE DAY of the ball at Le Ranelagh drew near, and Basile was at last allowed to leave the morning of. The king had not once requested a private interview with him, which meant he had only wished to be assured of Basile's fealty. He had to field a few questions about the nature of his betrothal from the overly inquisitive, but he mostly kicked his heels as he waited to get back to see Sophie.

It was strange that he should be eager to see her, as though they were betrothed in truth. But he could not deny his anticipation. The king at last questioned him about his wish to attend the ball, allowing him to admit he had bought an annual subscription, and that he had made plans to attend before having the pleasure of waiting upon his king. He was then graciously given leave to go and make himself ready. Upon arriving at his house in Paris, he decided to dash off a word to Sophie to tell her of his liberty to accompany her.

On impulse, before he sealed the letter, he added that if she wished to dress in the style of the French with hair powdered white and more color on her face, Jeannot would be skilled enough to help her.

That evening, Basile attended to his appearance more carefully than usual. Leaving the restraints of Versailles must surely have contributed to his exuberance in attending the ball. It was too early in the court's mourning period to wear the ivory and golds he preferred, so it would have to be black. But he would wear a white shirt and neckcloth along with the gray breeches and clocked stockings. He had a small collection of wigs, and he wore them when at Versailles. But his hair was thick enough that he could powder it and pull it back and still be considered to have dressed with elegance. He wondered if Sophie would allow Jeannot to assist her as he had suggested.

He brought his carriage to Zoé's house to fetch her, her sister, and mother—M. Sainte-Croix had taken unwell and could not attend. They stopped at Sophie's house next, and there, he bid the ladies to wait in the carriage while he went in to escort her. A light rain had begun to fall, but having brought an umbrella, he was prepared. He hoped it would not spoil their evening.

At his rap on the door, the maid admitted him, and in a matter of moments, he was standing in the entranceway. At the sound of his arrival, Sophie exited from one of the rooms, dressed in a magnificent Parisian gown of dove gray. As for the rest, Jeannot had evidently seen to Sophie's *toilette*.

Her hair was pulled up higher than usual, brushed over some sort of cushion as was the fashion. A large curl fell over her shoulder, and the *boucles*—the curls on each side of her face—framed the most charming expression. It was one of brown eyes, large with apprehension, and a shy smile that betrayed her anticipation. Her hair was powdered white, and the lovely cinnamon-clove scent of mareschal powder reached him, mingling with her usual scent of oranges. Her face had only the slightest dusting, but the red on her lips….

Ah, but he must not think of that when he would not be kissing them.

"You are *merveilleuse*, mademoiselle." Basile bowed low, then reached into his pocket for a small case. "Would you permit me?" He let his question dangle as he slid a tiny black patch in the shape of a heart into his fingers and approached her.

She stilled as he neared her, and his own breath ceased as he placed the patch on a spot just above where her dimple appeared when she smiled. He allowed his thumb to press the patch onto her cheek as his fingers grazed just underneath her chin. A strange stirring in his heart made it difficult to step away, and he had to wrench himself back.

"There. That will do nicely I think." His voice was gruff and he cleared it, cocking his head as he studied her. "You look French."

"Do I?" Her brown eyes opened slowly and she blinked at him. "That is a high compliment. I am aware my English fashion cannot compare to the Parisians'." Her eyes crinkled suddenly as she smiled at him.

"Zoé, Jeanne, and Madame Sainte-Croix await us in the carriage," he said, crooking his arm for her to slip hers through it.

She turned back to bid farewell to Mary just as Jeannot came into the corridor. The nurse greeted the marquis with an affectionate pat on his cheek and promised to take good care of Mrs. Twisden.

"Thank you, Jeannot—and for assisting me with my hair," Sophie said, turning back to smile at the nurse.

Basile helped her into the carriage and participated in the excited chatter as they bowled away in the direction of Passy. His thoughts, however, did not stray far from the vision of Sophie and her red-stained lips, or the feel of her skin under his fingers. He would have to make sure they had plenty of time at the ball to dance together and to talk. They still had not coordinated the stories of their supposed engagement.

The rain had ceased by the time the carriage deposited them at the entrance to the ball. There, they followed the crowd through the arched entrance, and once inside the walled space, Basile glanced around, impressed despite himself. The interior was as lavish as though it were the inside of the opera house, although the night sky was visible with all its stars beyond the multitude of lustres, each with a lit candle. The vestibule contained arcades in between a series of pilasters, and the last arcade on the left held a space to deposit hats and canes.

"Would you look at that," Sophie breathed.

Farther inside, each wall was adorned with ionic columns painted in the color of marble, whose bases were each done in pale blue. Beyond the columns was a covered walkway with benches upon which to sit, and on each side of the floor were massive chimneys adorned with mirrors. At the end of the promenade was a sunken dance floor with more benches to provide an amphitheater that looked out over it. And the whole of the place was brightly lit from candelabras and chandeliers. Everyone present was dressed in the height of fashion, though the sober colors still reigned.

The Sainte-Croix family immediately found acquaintances and fell into conversation with them, and Basile was able to lead Sophie to the side of the room.

"I was unsure if you would return in time for the ball until I got your message," Sophie said as they settled on one of the benches.

"I was as unsure as you, for the king had given me no indication if and when I might leave." He smiled at her, finding her *mignonne*, elaborately attired thus. What made her cute he could not say, except that perhaps it did not seem as though a veiled expression were possible on her face when she had the adorable patch next to her red lips.

She bit those lips now, and he detected anxiety in her expression. "Basile, I fear there is a complication to our sham betrothal."

He immediately thought of the queen and wondered if Sophie could possibly have heard of their conversation in the drawing room. He decided not to tell her of it if she had not. It would only increase that look of anxiety.

"Tell me," he said.

She closed her lips and breathed in deeply. "Sheldon is planning to present you with the bills for our expenses in Paris—our lodging, my gowns—everything!" She closed her eyes.

Basile broke his stunned silence with an audible gasp, then, "*Le diable l'emporte!*"

The devil take him!

She regarded him with unease, but he merely laughed with incredulity. "The peacock has no elegance of mind. You are well rid of him." She kept her eyes on him, and he could see she was not reassured, so he shook his head. "Let him hand me all of your bills and think no more of it. It is true that I should not choose to act as he did in the same circumstance, but there is no reason why you should be punished for his infamy."

Her eyes quit his as she trained her gaze forward. "I can understand his frustration with me, although it is most certainly not of my doing. But it is most humiliating."

A dance set was forming in front of them, and Basile made a split decision. Sophie needed to dance just now and toss her cares away. There was no reason not to enjoy this evening, or their sham betrothal—as she called it—to the fullest.

"You need be under no obligation to that man. I will stand your friend." He smiled at her, and held out his hand. "Come. Let us join this set."

CHAPTER 10

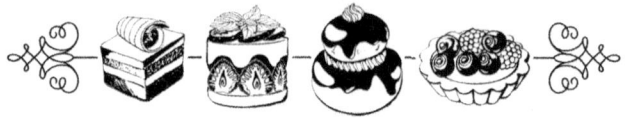

Sophie followed Basile onto the dance floor and took her position across from him in the line, curtsying to her partner as the minuet began. She had never been more upended by her circumstances than she was now. Here she was in a foreign country, supposedly betrothed to a man who possessed a title and was in a station far above her own, vulnerable and exposed, dependent upon him for finances and her reputation—her grandmother unable to guide or shield her, her only English friend proving himself to be no friend at all. She was astonished that she was not prostrate from the anxiety of her situation.

She slipped her hand into his, their stares locked as she moved in pattern to the next partner. She could feel his eyes on her when she left his hands. Sophie had always thought herself independent, a woman who knew her own mind. But all that she had thought quite firm and unshakable within her dismantled under his touch. Earlier in her house, when he had stepped close to press a patch upon her cheek, she could not breathe. Could not move until he released her from his touch. It was an inexplicable emotion to be so helpless when he drew near. It could not be love—it was much too soon to declare such a thing. It must simply be attraction.

And he was attractive. Not only in physical appearance —indeed he was that—but in charisma. There was a magnetism about him that pulled her toward him—pulled her eyes, pulled her arm into his, pulled her person to draw near until she had established herself firmly at his side. Oh, she was in grave danger of giving her heart to the man if she was not careful. For he could never be anything more to her than a charming acquaintance she once knew in Paris.

Regardless of how much she questioned her attraction to him, she could not question his trustworthiness. He might be a liar, for all she knew. He might be impoverished, a gentleman of no consequence who ingratiated himself into French society, but...

But no. That was impossible. Basile was who he said he was. Besides what society and his friends said of him, he just wasn't someone who seemed false.

He bowed to her at the end of their dance and brought her to Zoé's mother and sister just as Zoé and her partner returned, her eyes sparkling. "Sophie, do you know Mr. Arlington?"

The Englishman greeted Sophie by bowing before her. "Indeed, we have not had that pleasure. How do you do?"

She murmured a suitable reply, and Zoé leaned in to whisper something to him. Sophie watched them, struck now by what she saw was a clear partiality on both sides. He listened intently to what Zoé said, allowing himself to linger before standing upright to return his gaze to Sophie. Zoé's attention was pulled by her sister.

"Mademoiselle Sainte-Croix informs me that you are

betrothed to Monsieur le Marquis de Verdelle." Mr. Arlington glanced in Basile's direction where he had gone in search of refreshments. "I had heard that he was betrothed to an Englishwoman but did not know who until now. I must congratulate you. I understand the queen is in favor of your match and is eager to meet you."

"Wh...what?" Sophie's breath left her at once. The queen? Marie-Antoinette? How had she even heard of it? Basile surely would not have announced it.

Before she could answer, Mr. Arlington smiled reassuringly. "Yesterday, Lord Stormont was invited to have an audience with her, and it was there that he learned of the beautiful Englishwoman." He darted a glance at Zoé's back. "Those were the queen's words. That a beautiful Englishwoman had captured the heart of an elusive French marquis. The whole court is talking of it."

Zoé turned from her conversation with her sister and caught the last part. Something in Mr. Arlington's words seemed to strike her as funny, and she hid her smile behind her fan.

Basile returned, delivering a glass of Champagne to Sophie. He then noticed Zoé empty-handed, surrendered his own glass to her, and looked around at the awkward silence. "What did I miss?"

"The queen knows of our betrothal?" Sophie asked him, fear creeping up her spine. She did not know precisely what she feared. Oh, everything, she supposed. She was so wholly out of her element in this country and in this dangerous game they were playing.

"Ah." Basile looked chagrined and glanced at Mr. Arlington. "You had it from the ambassador?" When Mr. Arlington nodded, he turned back to her. "Indeed. I do not know how she knew, but she is remarkably well connected.

Someone must have been at Madame Beauchamp's dinner, whose task it is to report back to her anything of an interesting nature."

Sophie waited for him to elaborate—to reassure her—but he merely shrugged. "It is of no account. I gave her a brief recital of our meeting and hinted that it was *un véritable coup de foudre*."

"I always told you that when at last you fell in love, it would be a case of love at first sight," Zoé said, her mirth escaping in a giggle. Mr. Arlington studied her, his serious expression close to a frown. He must have wondered what about it made Zoé laugh, but then, he did not know it was not a true engagement. It also seemed he could not entirely hide the jealous feelings he held toward the marquis. That she could understand. Basile and Zoé were so close as to cause anyone with a particular interest to wonder if they might cherish secret feelings for one another. She would be tempted to be jealous as well except that she had no cause to be, for she had no real claim whatsoever on Basile.

Basile stopped Zoé from elaborating with a look, and something of an understanding passed between them that did not serve to alleviate Mr. Arlington's suspicions, for he soon took a cold leave of Zoé.

As soon as he was gone, her face fell. "I do not understand Englishmen. They just grow reserved and pull back their affection the minute they are no longer the center of a woman's attention. Why is that?" She turned to Sophie suddenly. "How can any woman give her undivided attention to one man?"

Sophie glanced at her in surprise. "I...I do not know." She thought of the men of her acquaintance. Sheldon would certainly not pull back his attention when a woman wasn't interested. He would only increase it until he was bludgeoning her to death by his regard. In fact, she wished he would pull back. "Perhaps it is only that he feels strongly—"

She stopped herself. She did not wish to voice her suspicions about the nature of Mr. Arlington's interest, although Zoé seemed far from being offended by her familiarity.

Sophie tried again. "I could not help but notice that perhaps the two of you harbor a...preference for one another? And yet—if you will forgive me for frank speaking—you do not appear to return his feelings in a way that would cast out all doubt. I believe some men are proud and will withdraw their heart rather than risk their affection not being returned."

Zoé lowered her eyes, her lips straightening in a firm line. "That shows no courage at all. Perhaps such men are not worth fighting for, then. Why should a woman cease to enjoy herself for fear that a man might decide her smiles are too easily given?"

Sophie glanced at Basile, who was watching her. His face was absent of its usual glint of humor as though he were truly curious about her answer.

"You may be right," she said cautiously. "But those same men might very well fight for a woman's heart if only they are assured of their love being returned. Wholeheartedly, faithfully, and with a single focus."

She glanced back at Basile, and his lowered eyelids made it impossible to discern what he was thinking or whether he thought her advice sound. In the next moment, one of Zoé's admirers came to join the circle and carried her away for a dance.

"Wholeheartedly, faithfully, and with a single focus," he said, smiling at Sophie until her breath evaporated. "I told Zoé something along the same lines, but it is much prettier having it come from your lips."

Sophie discovered how enjoyable it was to experience a ball at Basile's side. He left her at regular intervals as was fashionable, but she felt his steady presence and it brought her a sense of protection. And, miracle upon miracle, he was able to pull Zoé and her sister and mother away at little after midnight, claiming a long ride home.

The next morning, Sophie peeked into her grandmother's room and found her supported by cushions so she was able to sit partially upright. It was the first time her grandmother was seated thus and fully alert, and Sophie knew it was time to talk to her about the bills first and foremost, but also to tell her about the betrothal. As she entered the room, Jeannot patted her arm affectionately.

"I will leave you."

Sophie murmured her thanks, glancing after the nurse. She had not seemed to lose her remarkable energy even in the past days caring for Mrs. Twisden.

Returning her regard to her grandmother, Sophie came over and sat on the chair near her bedside. She clasped one of her hands and smiled at her. "You look well."

"I do feel improved. But it is too soon to think of leaving the bed, as much as I would like to."

"Much too soon," Sophie replied, admonition touching her voice. "I am too thankful to see you recovering to wish for you to relapse into another bout of illness."

"I can't believe I have wasted so much of our precious

time in Paris by being bed-bound." Her grandmother sighed.

She reached her other hand out and Sophie understood she wished for water, which Jeannot had managed to infuse with lemon. The nurse had taken the morning to return to the marquis's house and replenish her stock from the greenhouse there. Sophie owed a debt of gratitude to the marquis she would not be able to pay.

When her grandmother had finished drinking, she handed the glass back to Sophie and asked, "How is our Sheldon doing? I hope he has managed to find enough to amuse himself with in Paris. He agreed to this trip as a great favor to me. Otherwise, I think he would never bestir himself to leave England."

"As to that," Sophie began, her brows knit, "is it true that he not only arranged the trip, but also financed it?"

Mrs. Twisden sent Sophie a startled glance, then dropped her eyes. "So you know about that. I meant to tell you."

She fell silent and when Sophie grew tired of waiting for more, she prompted her. "Why did you do it? Of course Sheldon has expectations of marriage if he is purchasing my gowns and everything else on this journey."

Irritation had seeped into her voice, and she did not wish to be irritated with her grandmother. She was the only person Sophie had left on this earth, but this incautious agreement to allow Sheldon to foot their bills seemed most unlike her.

"Sheldon proposed it when I confessed I wished to go to Paris but had not the means. At the beginning, he did not bring up the idea of marriage as a consequence, and I assumed he had decided to help because of his friendship with your father. When I understood his intentions in your regard, it was too late to pull back. I had hoped you might develop feelings in return..." She raised guilty eyes to Sophie. "Do not think too harshly of me, my dear."

Sophie could not like that her grandmother had done this without talking to her, but she could not remain angry or even judge her. How could she, when she had her own secrets?

She shook her head. "I don't."

"I am glad to hear it." Her grandmother squeezed her hand. Then, after a pause, she added, "How is he keeping himself?"

Sophie fingered the coverlet and studied the pattern of red flowers and green foliage printed onto the cream fabric. It was now that she needed to open up in the same way she wished her grandmother had done with her. But she could not be entirely truthful, for to confess that she had pretended an engagement she had no hope of keeping—only to make it perfectly clear that Sheldon had no hope of winning her hand—would only plunge her grandmother into worry. It provided only a temporary relief and solved nothing.

"As to Sheldon," she began. She bit her lip and looked at her grandmother, whose careworn face she loved so much. Her eyes had dimmed with illness but were still studying her as intelligently as ever.

Sophie wondered what she could say that would be honest but not force her to confess what she was not ready to. "Sheldon does seem to be enjoying himself in Paris, for he has a number of engagements that keep him occupied."

"I am much relieved to hear it," Mrs. Twisden said, as if that settled it. "My dear, would you brush my hair for me? I do not like to bother Mary when she is so busy, and I fear to tax Jeannot with it when she is only here as a favor to us."

Sophie nodded and took the brush, its bristles softened with use. She removed her grandmother's cap and brushed the long silver hair that had greatly thinned with age but was still beautiful.

"I have some news that will quite surprise you, I think," she said cautiously, thankful that she was not forced to look at her grandmother as she said it.

"Is that so?"

"Yes, for I am to be married." Her voice faltered then. How could she tell her grandmother the particulars of such a falsehood?

"Do you mean that despite everything you *have* accepted Sheldon?" Mrs. Twisden struggled to turn to look at her, so Sophie dropped her arm and met her regard. She sat on the bed and took her grandmother's hand.

"It is not Sheldon." She smiled, or rather struggled to smile. "It is the marquis. Monsieur Gervain. The man who brought us Jeannot."

Mrs. Twisden's expression was confused until she connected Basile with his nurse and then her confusion turned to amazement. "The marquis? But...you hardly know him! How did you manage to...to catch his interest?"

"I can scarcely say," Sophie said, blushing from embarrassment and chagrin at deceiving her grandmother. Borrowing a line from Zoé, she said, "I believe it must have been love at first sight between us."

"Well, well." Her grandmother absorbed that. Then, after a short reflection, she smiled suddenly. "I own that I am sorry for Sheldon, for he must be experiencing some disappointment, but I can only rejoice for you, my dear. How did it come about?"

Sophie thought back to their meeting outside of Stohrer. "I believe there was an understanding between us as soon as we met that allowed us to reach an agreement so quickly." What she said was so close to the truth that her heart pained her at the idea that this was not a true betrothal. "But I do not want for you to be overly excited, Grandmama. I wished to tell you, but not to focus on it at present. I would like to have you recover fully."

"And then we may plan the nuptials," her grandmother said with a smile. "I *am* rather tired."

"Yes, then we may plan the nuptials," Sophie repeated, the ache in her heart taking on greater proportions. "Let me remove this pillow so you may sleep more comfortably.

She did so and kissed her grandmother's forehead before leaving the room and shutting the door quietly behind her. She would do anything to spare her grandmother worry, even if it meant shielding her from the truth. She had to make sure the engagement was believable, and only when her grandmother was fully recuperated and ready to return home would they go about enacting the break of their sham agreement.

CHAPTER 11

Basile strolled into the Procope café where he found Grégoire and Armand sitting over coffee and brandy. On his way to their table, M. Necker raised his hand in greeting from where he sat nearby with the *philosophes* before calling out to him.

"You are the talk of the town, *mon cher* marquis. You've managed to draw the queen's eye, despite the royal period of mourning, and relieve its monotony with your engagement."

Basile did not quite know how to respond to such…was it praise? He was not given to flowery speech, though it was almost a requirement of the court. He nodded his head in thanks, then took the chair at his friends' table.

"Monsieur Necker is right," Armand said. "We have been hounded with questions from everyone who knows us to be your intimates. What is your objective with this whole affair? I know you had no marital intentions a week ago. Do you mean to marry her in earnest?"

Grégoire sipped his brandy, murmuring wickedly, "I

told him you had succumbed at last, although perhaps less to love than a desire to flee La Bordenave."

"But I cannot see how you can announce a betrothal publicly and not go through with it," Armand continued in an urgent undertone. "I will not believe it of you."

Basile lifted his hand to signal a waiter for coffee. "Tell us of your own courtship, Armand. Mine carries so little interest."

Armand creased his brow at the change of subject, but a smile played about his lips. "I have gained an audience with Vivienne's older brother, and he seems pleased by the match, although we have yet to discuss contracts."

"Allow me to congratulate you." Basile reached for the sugar and placed a lump in the cup of coffee that was set before him.

"It seems we are to wish you happy at last," Grégoire added.

"To think that she would notice me." Armand smiled again dreamily, a man clearly smitten. Grégoire told him he was much too modest.

Basile opened his mouth to ask Grégoire if he had sold his hunter, but Armand would not be put off from his earlier interrogation. "However, let us not detract from your engagement. Why did you do it?"

Basile stirred the sugar, contemplating his answer. "It was in both of our best interests to declare a false engagement, for it allowed me to shake off the widow and her to be spared the unwelcome attention of the Englishman, Cholmsley. Trust me, the lady has no intentions of holding me to it," he replied with a confidence he was far from feeling.

"As to La Bordenave," Armand said, "she has been asking many questions regarding your supposed meeting and how your understanding came to be. I do not comprehend how a woman can be so persistent when all hope is lost." He pulled out a box of his snuff and offered it to Grégoire, then Basile. "I believe I answered her questions well, but it was not an easy matter. I repeated that you had known each other in England. That is not true, is it?"

The café was loud and no one nearby paid them any attention, so Basile did not fear answering. He shook his head. "Our little arrangement is merely a means to bring relief to both of us in certain quarters. There will be no harm in ending it when the time comes."

"Not even when the queen is anxious to follow your betrothal and see you wed?" Grégoire asked, *sotto voce*.

"Not even then. She shall console me on our divergent paths and turn her attention elsewhere," Basile answered hopefully, but the conversation was growing uncomfortable as it forced a truth he would rather not face. Extricating himself from the betrothal might prove more difficult than he'd imagined now that more people were becoming involved.

Another truth slinked into his consciousness that was difficult to face. A part of him wondered if he wished to be freed.

The Duc d'Orleans entered the café and the proprietor set down a tray he was wiping to come and greet him with a bow. "Monsieur, you will perhaps wish to come with me. There is a gentleman who has been asking after you particularly."

"A creditor?" the duke asked.

"None other," the proprietor replied. "Allow me to show you to the back entrance so you may avoid him."

"You are most kind." The duke followed him to a door that led to a small cobblestone passageway in the back.

This was one reason the Procope was so popular amongst their set. With a benevolent owner, they were unlikely to be dunned by creditors there, for none could catch them.

Grégoire touched Basile on the arm, pulling his attention back. "You may wish to know that contrary to Armand's belief that he threw La Bordenave off the scent, she has let it be known publicly that she does not believe your betrothal to be true."

Basile shrugged. "It is her problem, is it not?"

"Except that now the queen's former rival, Madame Du Barry, has been cast off, Claudia is working hard to win Marie-Antoinette's favor. If the queen gets wind of the widow's accusations, she might have more questions for you. Questions you will not be able to avoid and will be hard-pressed to answer without deepening your falsehoods. And if she has doubts, she will not rest until she is satisfied with your intentions." Grégoire glanced at Armand, who knew the way of the court better than anyone. "Is that not so?"

"I am in complete agreement." Armand thought for a minute. "Everyone seems to question how thoroughly the Englishwoman has captured your heart and whether your engagement is as fixed as you say it is. I suggest you bring your flirtation with her into the public eye to prove them wrong—a task I trust you will not find too onerous."

No, he would not find it onerous. But how had things come to such a pass where it was *he* taking love advice from Armand?

Basile had no difficulty in securing an invitation for Sophie to the following night's soirée at the Lemoines'. He sent it along with a handwritten note explaining that the invitation was for a casual supper followed by drawing room conversation with the most influential of French society. It would be the ideal place, he explained, for them to show Mr. Cholmsley and everyone else how besotted they were with one another if she were of a mind to agree to the farce. There appeared to be some doubt about their betrothal, and it would behoove them to prove the skeptics otherwise. He did not wish to cause her any disquiet, but thought it better that they were agreed upon how to proceed.

Despite telling himself he was doing the right thing in urging her to a more outward display of their supposed affection, he suffered some small anxiety waiting for his footman to return with her response.

Mon cher Basile, it said.

I have not heard from Sheldon Cholmsley in two days, so I do not know if he will be in attendance to witness our display, but I will certainly come and assist you in dispelling those injurious rumors. Je t'embrasse, Sophie.

He smiled at her teasing tone about the injurious rumors, thankful that she was capable of humor. At least, he was fairly certain she was being humorous. But then she had closed with, "I kiss you" in his own language, as though they were indeed friends. The words went straight to his heart despite the careful barricades he had put around it. He imagined placing a kiss on one cheek, then turning to the other cheek and kissing her there. Then drawing center...

No. Absolutely not. He could not lead her on a false path

of forcing a betrothal that he said would be just for show, only to then toy with her heart by kissing her. That would be most ungentlemanly. Almost as bad as presenting another man with a bill that he himself had promised to honor.

That night, he left off the powder, imagining that Sophie would also appear in more simple attire. He used the excuse of their betrothal to fetch her himself without Zoé. As much as he loved Zoé, she would fill every silence so that he could hardly enjoy Sophie's presence.

As he reached for the knocker to her house, the door of the adjoining house opened, and Cholmsley stepped out. He scowled as soon as he saw Basile.

Basile swallowed the biting words he was tempted to utter and bowed. "A pleasure, Monsieur Cholmsley."

"If you say so," the peacock replied. "I will be calling upon you with a business matter in a day or two, if you would be good enough to give me your direction."

Basile reached into the pocket of his waistcoat and drew out one of his cards. He handed it to him unsmilingly. "You may have it, although I am not in the habit of discussing... business, as you call it, with gentlemen I scarcely know," he replied.

"This business concerns you nearly," Mr. Cholmsley replied before giving a curt nod and striding over to a carriage that was being held for him in front of Basile's chaise.

He watched him drive off and shook his head. For the first time it occurred to him that he could not leave Sophie to return to England on her own, and he certainly couldn't leave her to that man's care. He would have to take her home himself, which would cause tongues to wag unless he were able to do it discreetly. He touched the cold brass knocker and lifted it, pausing. He would not mind the journey in her presence, though. She seemed unlikely to create the sort of fuss that would make such a trip arduous, and it would give him pleasure to extend their acquaintance.

Mary opened the door at his knock, where inside Sophie was waiting for him. Her hair was dressed more simply, the powder scarcely visible, but her gown was new and decidedly French. It was made up of dark gray silk with black embroidery on the stomacher, and the cut of the bodice pulled her shoulders back sharply and nipped in her waist. Her sleeves were lightly puffed with white ribbons at the end, and white lace trimmed the low-cut bodice. If her face was powdered, this, too, was scarcely visible. As much as he'd been impressed by her beauty when she had put effort into wearing Paris fashions, he was struck as he gazed at her naked face now. This was a face he could grow to admire deeply.

He bowed to cover the distraction of these thoughts and held out his arm to assist her out of doors and into the waiting carriage.

"So, Monsieur le Marquis," she said when she had settled herself comfortably, "what is to be our plan? What sort of flirtation are you suggesting?"

From her smile, Sophie did not seem to be worried he meant anything inappropriate. Her faith in him was rather remarkable. She had trusted him enough to pretend to know one another upon a mere glance. She had trusted him when he announced their betrothal to the society at large without having given her warning ahead of time. And even now, she was agreeing to allow him to escort her alone in his carriage so they might discuss plans for a bolder flirtation under public scrutiny. Her expression was full of trust.

Basile smiled at her, his eyes softening at such a display of innocence. "Let us say that I shall permit myself—with your full agreement, of course—to slip my fingers under that charming *boucle* that hangs down onto your neck." She was again wearing the full curl that Jeannot had coaxed to life the night of the Ranelagh, ball which came down from the left side of her coiffure and rested on her shoulder, spilling over onto her collarbone.

"Touching my neck in the process, I assume," she said, pink with an innocent embarrassment but pluck for the challenge.

"I shall endeavor to restrict my graze of your shoulder to all that is correct," he replied, keeping his tone light, but noticing at the same time a desire to loosen his collar.

"Tickling me and causing the most unattractive goose flesh to erupt over my arms, I suppose. And what else?" she demanded.

He examined her. "I may be called upon to sit directly beside you so that our shoulders and legs are very near." As he said it, his knee grazed hers in the dark of the carriage as though it had a will of its own. "When I am standing, I might lean in close and whisper into your ear."

"Whereupon I laugh most delightedly at what you have just said, proving at once that you are the most diverting man I have ever met and that we share such confidences as to leave no doubt regarding our engagement. You behold in me a woman properly enthralled."

"It is only natural," he replied, his lips curling up of their own accord, "for I am French."

"And therefore a most practiced flirt besides being excessively diverting," she replied. "I see. And what else?"

Basile thought for a moment. "I may be required from time to time to offer a small kiss on your cheek. Perhaps in the area where I placed your patch, there"—he lifted his finger to touch her cheek—"on that dimple next to your mouth."

Sophie's emotions were betrayed in her nervous laugh. "Of course. I shall endeavor to endure it while showing a suitable mix of bashfulness and delight."

"Delight you will be far from feeling, of course," he could not but add in a teasing voice, hoping it were not so.

She met his stare quite frankly. "Oh, I would not go so far as to say that. But Basile—"

The use of his given name in their intimate setting reminded him of their charade, and he wondered if she was thinking the same thing. She had stopped short, and he was forced to prod her. "What is it?"

Her look grew vulnerable, but she shrugged it off. "'Tis nothing. I am perfectly ready to follow you in this charade, for it suits my own ends. Sheldon has not been by to visit once since I assured him I was serious in my determination to marry you. However, if we are seen to be too affectionate, it might give rise to a different sort of talk—one I would not at all like to have said about me, particularly when I return to England unmarried."

She averted her gaze, entreating softly, "Do not carry the flirtation too far." And although he could not be quite sure of it, he thought he heard her add, "For it will only confuse me."

Basile reached out for her hand and she placed it in his. "I am a gentleman, and I will do nothing to harm your reputation. *En plus*, you may be sure that I will see you safely returned to England when your time here is finished, although it cannot be until the king has given me leave to quit the territory."

She slipped her hand out of his and clasped hers on her

lap. The gesture left him frowning—wondering if he had carried everything too far.

"Tell me again," he said. "Are you certain you can accept that our betrothal is false? I plunged you into a difficult situation by announcing our engagement without first gaining your accord. I must insist that I will do the honorable thing and marry you, even without the pressure of society forcing such a thing by their talk."

She smiled and shook her head, her eyes fixed on her fingers knit together. "I would not wish a marriage for such reasons. As much as I will not marry for convenience, nor will I marry to still gossiping tongues. I merely hope to avoid particularly ruinous slander."

She looked up and smiled at him in the dark of the carriage as it began to slow. The sounds of other carriages and people's voices grew louder, signaling they had arrived at their destination.

"Do you know," she said, "there is a dower house on the edge of my family's property that was bequeathed to me? I believe that I would happily live in the most frugal manner there rather than marry for any reason other than love. The kind of love where—"

Basile held his breath waiting for the rest. She opened her lips, but the footman had hopped down and opened the door to the carriage, so Basile had no choice but to step out and give his hand to assist her to alight. He would not know the rest—*now*. But he would find it out, for he'd thought there were only two kinds of love. An unrequited desperate kind or a wedded love in name but entirely devoid of passion. He suspected she had spoken of neither.

CHAPTER 12

The Lemoines' soirée was not as intimate as Basile had suggested in his note. He and Sophie trailed behind a stream of people who greeted their hosts before following the crowd upstairs. She assumed if he had invited her to it, the most notable of society would be in attendance and that was all that was needed for their ruse. It did cross her mind briefly to wonder why either of them were so fixed upon keeping up the appearances of their engagement, but that involved examining motivations she was not quite ready to face, so she put it out of her mind.

It was their turn, and Basile greeted the host and hostess before introducing her as his charming fiancée.

"Of whom we have heard so much," Madame Lemoine said with a kind smile as Sophie curtsied. "I hope you will enjoy yourself this evening."

The Lemoines lived near the Palais Royale and their house was the largest she had yet seen in Paris. They were shown up to the drawing room on the first floor, which felt spacious despite the number of people congregating there.

In an adjoining room, tables were laid out with a spread of delicacies and *amuse-bouches* that would be simple to eat with one's fingers.

Basile leaned in to whisper in her ear, stirring the tiny hairs on her neck and causing her to startle, then hold her breath from his nearness. The smooth silk of his coat brushed her arm and his warmth caused heat to rush through her. Somehow, she had not expected him to start his plan of flirtation so soon.

"If I leave your side for a moment, can you bear it? The duke is signaling his desire to speak to me, and he is not someone I wish to put in your path. He is something of a *roué*."

She tucked her head to the side to answer him in a like manner without pulling quite as close as he had. "It may surprise you to know that I do not fear being left alone in a room full of foreigners. Although," she added in a louder voice with a teasing grin, "it must tax every emotion to be parted from you, be it only for a moment."

A woman turned at her words, and Sophie recognized her as the widow Basile seemed to be trying to avoid. He returned the smile, then left in an opposite direction from her. As soon as he'd gone, the woman came up to her—to cause trouble, no doubt. Sophie would not be easily cowed.

"Miss Twisden, is it?" the widow asked her in strongly accented English.

"It is. And I believe you are Madame Bordenave," Sophie replied, unperturbed by the sly hostility she heard in her tone.

"You know all, it seems." Madame Bordenave studied her for a moment. "So you have captured our marquis, and yet with such bland English looks and mannerisms. The

English race has always been an insipid one, has it not? It is astonishing that a warm-blooded Frenchman could look your way."

Sophie was not as beautiful as Madame Bordenave, she knew. But such spitefulness did nothing to add to the widow's beauty.

"I suppose you wish to provoke some sort of retaliatory feeling in me, but I am sorry to disoblige you," Sophie said. "As insipid as the English might be, *something* about me in particular has drawn your marquis, as you have said. I can only suppose that he does not find anything bland about me at all."

Madame Bordenave stared hard at her. "If he brings you to the altar, perhaps I might concur. But there has not even been a *repas de fiançailles* announced."

An engagement dinner? Sophie was unaware that the French did such a thing after they became engaged. She must ask Basile. Before she could think of an answer, Madame Bordenave leaned nearer, overwhelming Sophie with the scent of patchouli.

"When he and I were engaged, that was the very first thing he did. He was *quite* eager to bring me to the altar, I assure you."

Every one of Sophie's nerves was on end in this battle of female wits. Why, *why* did some women feel it necessary to drag others down so they might pull themselves up, like a cock on a dung heap?

"Perhaps the engagement dinner *has* been announced, but only to those to whom it concerns," she suggested, a smile touching her lips. She was not afraid of the widow, but a cold settled in her stomach despite her fearlessness. Sophie did not wish to be humiliated by a woman such as she, and it was beginning to dawn on her that she would be if they were to announce their rupture before she left Paris. It was clear Madame Bordenave was roiling with jealousy.

"What I am most curious to know," Sophie went on, deciding it was better to go on the offensive than to stand back on her weak foot, "is why you are so single-mindedly throwing your heart after a lost cause. An engaged man? You have nothing to gain and everything to lose."

Madame Bordenave narrowed her eyes. "Allow me to inform you—"

"Sophie!"

She turned to see who had spoken, and raised her eyes to the tall, slim figure who stood before her. It was one of Basile's friends. She quickly racked her brain for his name and in an instant was all smiles. "Grégoire, how lovely to see you this evening."

He bowed deeply, then stood straight with a smile in place. "The pleasure is all mine. I was hoping to have a moment of your time." Then, bowing to the widow, he added, "Madame," before slipping his arm under Sophie's and leading her to the far corner of the room.

As they walked, he leaned down to murmur, "Forgive me for addressing you by your Christian name. I had to do so or that woman would know it all. Any close friend of Basile's must call you Sophie, for he would quickly make sure any fiancée of his was on intimate terms with his friends. It is Basile's way. And of course you must know that he has confided everything to Armand and to myself."

"I guessed as much since you were there when he announced it." She squeezed his arm. "I give you full leave to call me Sophie, even when we are out of earshot of the widow and anyone else we might need to convince." She laughed. "And I made free use of your name, you must remember, although for a panicked moment I feared I would not remember it."

He pulled her to sit on a sofa as the people walking by glanced at them with some curiosity. He did not, however, sit as close as Basile had promised he would, but rather kept to his end.

"Armand and I have been wondering how you are bearing up under the scrutiny that comes from Basile's announcement." His manner of speaking to her was kind despite his having the appearance of a severe and even somewhat taciturn man.

She held his regard and sighed, then lowered hers with a resigned smile. "You must not see me as a victim, although"—at this she did have to incline toward him so he would make out her words—"he did catch me by surprise by the unexpected and public nature of it."

Grégoire gave a silent laugh. "Basile is nothing if not spontaneous."

"Somehow *that* does not shock me." Grégoire laughed audibly this time, pulling more glances their way, and she continued. "When I supported my grandmother in her idea of coming to Paris, even going so far as to depend upon Mr. Cholmsley in his role of escort, I had not realized how difficult a position I would put myself in where he was concerned. I was in need of protection from unwelcome attention, and this"—she splayed her fingers to communicate the betrothal and all it entailed—"has given me what I needed. For the time being."

He nodded, then looked up as Basile advanced upon them.

"I must offer you my deepest gratitude for squiring *ma*

Sophie while I was talking to the duke." Basile bowed. "But now be gone. I wish to sit next to my woman."

Grégoire lifted an eyebrow in surprise and stood, taking a proper leave of Sophie. "Far be it from me to stand in the way of two people so clearly besotted."

Basile smiled at him as he walked away, then immediately shifted close enough so his leg was touching hers and his arm was flush against her own in a partial embrace. Sophie drew in a sharp breath, then quickly wiped the surprise from her face and forced a smile for those who were watching her.

"There is no time to waste," she murmured.

"None." He leaned in so that his muscular thigh was flush against hers, and she could feel his breath on her neck. Her pulse fluttered, and she feared her limbs would shake. They were beginning to already.

"Do not be afraid of me," Basile murmured. There was nothing seductive about his voice. If anything, he sounded determined. "This is for show, but I will not compromise you. You may rely upon me, for I promise to bring you safely through this farce."

She nodded and relaxed slightly, although she had a strange desire to blink the moisture away from her eyes when he called it a farce. A farce it was, though, she firmly reminded herself.

"What I wish to know," went the murmur, still close but now friendly, "is what you and my friend Greg spoke of while I was called away." He said Greg with a strongly rolled *r*.

She bit back a smile. She had thought him to be speaking in a friendly way, but if she didn't know better, she would call this jealousy.

"You should not concern yourself with what we spoke

of—especially when we were not sitting as closely as you and I are."

"Nevertheless, one must have a topic of conversation when one is murmuring in a lady's ear to convince the world at large that we are madly in love with one another."

"Ah." Goodness. Sophie was determined—*determined*—that she would not succumb to any sort of feelings for this Frenchman, who possessed more charm than any man had a right to. However, she did wish she had remembered to bring her fan.

"Let me whisper back then"—she turned her face in the direction of his neck for the purpose—"if only to assure you that your friend and I spoke of nothing. I hardly remember what we spoke of." She allowed her gaze to roam around the room and willed her trembling to cease.

"Come. That is a poor answer."

She felt his eyes as he watched her. Then she felt his approach as he slowly lifted a hand to caress the curl that hung over her shoulder.

Her breath ceased.

The movement and voices in the room clanged and boomed, though they sounded from far away.

And then his fingers skimmed her shoulder as he lifted the curl in his hand.

Please don't kiss my neck, she thought, *for I shall be undone by such a gesture.* Despite her internal pleas, she could not have moved for all the world.

He dropped the curl and shifted away suddenly, and she drew in a breath as would a person who surfaced from the deep, even as she felt a crimson flush rise to her cheeks. As she lifted her eyes, she found Sheldon watching her, his face contracted in lines of fury. It was the sight of him that allowed her to bring her breathing back to normal and her flush to die down. Yes, she was a willing party to this farce if only to set her life on her own terms. Marry she might do, but only for the deepest affection. Absolutely not out of necessity and certainly not upon the pressure of a man who thought he had rights.

CHAPTER 13

Basile rose early the morning after the Lemoines' supper. He was surprisingly awake considering how late he had gone to bed and how much he had tossed and turned as he tried to sleep. He decided to take his horse out and ride along the Champs Élysées toward Passy in the direction of where the Ranelagh ball was held. It would get him some exercise and fresh air and would perhaps take his mind off the unsettling realization that occurred to him last night.

He was attracted to Sophie Twisden. *Very* attracted.

What had started out as mere flirtation to satisfy those who doubted their betrothal had taken on a sudden shift when he found himself ensconced on the small sofa at her side, leaning in to whisper in her ear and drawing in her happy scent of orange citrus. Grazing the soft skin of her neck as he toyed with the curl that fell from her coiffure had been a mistake, for it only made him aware of how much he wanted to continue the exploration.

It was an unfortunate realization to come to at this point, for he was neither ready to settle down—excepting of course if she held him to his public declaration—nor was she a woman he could trifle with. These thoughts dogged his steps as he went to the courtyard and called for his groom to saddle a horse, the ones for riding all of the Kladrubers breed. The stables were conveniently located in his *hôtel de ville*, which he had to admit was one benefit of holding the title of marquis. If any one of his older brothers were still alive, Basile would have had to content himself with a rented mews several streets away from whatever much smaller house he would possess.

He rode out, wearing a cape to keep off the dust, then turned left to ride along the Seine before crossing over the Pont Royal to continue along the Tuileries. Other riders were about, but none that he knew. Most of the people were in carriages and appeared to have a specific destination in mind. As he allowed his horse to follow the border of the Tuileries, the sight of its leafy trees reminded him that he had not gone there in a while, and the cooling green would be a soothing contrast to the summer heat. It was a project for the next time he was on foot.

Ahead of him, he caught a glimpse of what he thought was a familiar figure walking toward the entrance to the Tuileries near the palace. Was he seeing things? He nudged his horse forward to see if it was indeed she or whether he was conjuring the person he most wished to see.

"Sophie!"

She turned and shielded her eyes from the sun coming up behind him as she looked up. Her face broke out into a smile of recognition.

"Basile, I would have thought you still asleep after our late night."

"I might say the same about you," he replied. "But it

appears you are not a woman who is easily fatigued if you are up already. Do you ride?"

"I don't have a horse in Paris, but I do ride when I can." She glanced at her maid who was waiting at the entrance to the garden. "I was just headed into the Tuileries for a walk."

"I would accompany you if I could, but I cannot bring the horse in. Perhaps we might walk together there another time. Or ride somewhere else, if you prefer it. I will lend you one of my mounts."

"It is most kind of you," she said. After a brief moment when their conversation stalled, she offered up a smile and turned to go.

He was reluctant to see her leave. "Sophie!" When she turned back, he added, "We have not decided upon our next *sortie* together. What shall it be?"

"Ah!" She thought for a moment, then moved back to where his horse stood and raised her eyes to him. "This is quite awkward to speak of and not at all a public outing, but my grandmother is asking that you come to see her, and I do not know how to gainsay her. She is speaking of organizing a *repas de fiançailles* as soon as she is well enough to do so. I understand this is what the French do?" At this last bit she cringed as though fearing his response. But how could she think he would mind? He had brought this fully upon himself—*and* her.

"An engagement dinner! I hadn't thought about that, but of course it must be expected." His horse leaned down to nibble at a purple plant that grew in the cracks of the stone wall beside him and he gave him rein as he thought. She spoke before he could.

"I told Madame Bordenave that we had already organized one, but that it was private. I had to think of something, for she seems to believe you will not bring me to the altar." She laughed, but in her blush he could see the awkwardness of her situation, and not for the first time did he question his sanity in the moment he'd made his impulsive declaration.

"That woman is intolerable." He pulled up on the reins, bringing his horse's head up. "Leave such matters to me. I shall see that everything is done properly that will cause neither doubt nor stain upon your reputation. And as for your grandmother, if it pleases you, you may tell her to expect me tomorrow afternoon if she is well enough to receive me."

Sophie smiled. "She will say she is well enough, but she is still weak. Therefore, I must ask you not to remain too long, for she will insist upon being dressed and receiving you in the sitting room, and I should not like her to fall into a relapse."

"I will take care." Basile bowed from his horse. "And I will take leave of you now. Enjoy your walk, *ma chère* Sophie."

After she had bid him farewell, he led his horse in a canter as quickly as he could to the end of the quay and turned westward to the Champs Elysées, where he could have the run he desperately needed. He allowed his mind to roam, despite the fact that in one fashion or another his thoughts always seemed to return to her.

Later, after Basile reentered the gates of his courtyard and handed the reins over to his groom, he went to change his clothes before heading to his study where a newspaper awaited him, along with his correspondence. This and a glass of claret would be just the way to spend the afternoon. He had only just sat when the sound of the knocker announced a visitor.

The *majordome* entered bearing the card of a M. Sheldon

Cholmsley. *Blasted peacock*. He had better get this interview over with.

"Show him in."

When M. Cholmsley entered his study, Basile stood and gave him a short bow of acknowledgement. "I presume you are here for those matters you wished to discuss with me?"

If he had thought to disconcert M. Cholmsley when the time came to handing over the bills Sophie had warned him about, he much mistook the man. M. Cholmsley sat in the chair Basile had indicated, then brought a pile of papers out of a leather carrier he had with him. He set the pile on the table in front of him.

"You may know that I have paid for Sophie and Mrs. Twisden's journey to France, which included not only their travel, accommodation, and food, but also their gowns and other fripperies. This, of course, was so they might mingle comfortably in French society." He looked at Basile. "You must be aware that Sophie has not a farthing to her name."

Basile studied him for a minute under hooded eyelids that did little to conceal the derision he felt. "I am aware that Sophie brings other assets to our union than money, of which I have no need."

"I am glad to hear it. Then you will not mind my presenting you with these bills that Sophie and her grandmother have incurred since the beginning of the journey."

"And if I should mind?" Basile asked. "What will you do then?"

M. Cholmsley's face took on a belligerent look which did nothing to render his visage more noble. "I shall make it clear to the English society residing in Paris that you are unwilling to care for her needs, which makes me wonder if you are earnest in your willingness to marry her. And I shall cease to pay the rent for their house, although I will not leave them without help. They may reside with me until I return to England."

"I will not hide from you," Basile said, finding it difficult to keep a rein on his temper, "that I find your behavior repulsive. You attempted to force a marriage upon Sophie though she made it clear she did not wish for it. And you now try to pawn off bills to others that you had promised to honor. This is not the behavior of a gentleman."

"I little care what opinion you have of me." But M. Cholmsley's purple cheeks as he drew himself upright belied his words. "I merely wish to say that if you are bent on marrying her, I would advise you to show it by taking charge of her expenses."

Basile sipped the claret his servant had brought him, offering nothing to M. Cholmsley. He would not be staying long enough to drink it.

"You really are a man of coarse manners," Basile said in a mild voice. He had trained himself not to show his emotions so easily, but this one stretched his self-control thin. "A French gentleman does not discuss money in the way that you seem to be able to do."

He stood and sifted through some papers on his desk. "Here are the directions of my man of business. You may discuss this with him, although I am not entirely sure of his proficiency in the English tongue. Afterwards, I will instruct him on what I wish to do, once I've heard his opinion on the matter."

"I quite thought we might settle this here—"

"But we will not." Basile felt no compunction about cutting the visit short.

His manner seemed to infuriate the peacock, which of course it was calculated to do. M. Cholmsley gathered the papers and stuffed them back into his leather pouch, along with the card for the man of business.

"I do not believe that a betrothal so hastily arranged—and this between a man and woman from two different cultures—can possibly succeed. I do not know what game you are playing, but I hardly think you will end up marrying her after so short an acquaintance."

"You forget," Basile interjected with a raised eyebrow. "It has been two years since we first met."

"Then she will have second thoughts about leaving behind her country and yoking herself to a foreigner." M. Cholmsley lifted a finger. "Sophie is a weak woman and will be overset by this change in lifestyle. These complications will surely occur to her at some point before her marriage."

"Sophie, weak? You do not know her, then." Basile walked over to the door. "As you have nothing of good sense to say, I will bid you good day."

The door opened as he was about to reach for it. His *majordome* knew him well and must have sensed his dislike for the Englishman. He had not quit his post.

"You may show Monsieur Cholmsley out," he said.

Basile turned, and his visitor clutched his carrier in his right hand and shoved his cocked hat over his wig before stalking out of the room.

When he left, Basile looked at his servant. "I must pen a note to my *homme d'affaires* and will bid you to send someone to bring it to him."

His servant nodded, and Basile went over to his desk. He would instruct his man of business to provide whatever financial relief Sophie and her grandmother might need and give instructions about the payment of their current and future bills. However, he was undecided over the course of action regarding the bills from before their engagement which M. Cholmsley wished to pass over to him. He would let his man of business do the negotiations. After all, as he'd said to M. Cholmsley, a gentleman did not discuss such affairs.

THE NEXT DAY, Basile presented himself at Sophie's door and glanced at the adjoining house where Cholmsley lived. The sight brought his ire back in full force. For the briefest of moments, his irritation against the man turned into frustration over how this engagement was complicating his life. However, when the more egotistical portion of his brain tried to lay the burden at Sophie's door, he stopped himself.

She had not entrapped him. She had not even remarked his presence until he had forced himself upon her notice. No. There was only one person to blame, and it was he, himself. He had brought this on his own head, and he would cheerfully do whatever was necessary to extricate both Sophie and himself from the mess.

He rapped at the door and waited until Mary opened it. After delivering a curtsy and a smile more friendly than the maid had thus far given him, she led him to the sitting room where he found Sophie seated in one of her more colorful gowns. Mourning attire could be dispensed with if one was just sitting at home. Her grandmother sat near her, similarly attired.

As he bowed deeply before Mrs. Twisden, he noticed that she looked as though she had been brought back from death's door, although wild dogs could not have dragged the truth from him. Whatever color her fever must have lent her had given way to a pasty complexion that held a yellowish tint. Her hair was done neatly but her dress hung from her slim frame, and she trembled as he released the hand he had taken when he bowed.

"Your servant, Madame Twisden," he said. "You are looking the picture of health, I am pleased to see."

"You are a flatterer, but I would prefer that over the truth at the moment. Please sit." Her smile was severe and her voice frail as she gestured to the chair, showing how much the visit cost her. Sophie was seated on the edge of hers as though ready to leap up should her grandmother need her. But Mrs. Twisden was still an admirable old woman despite her infirmity. It gave him a glimpse of where Sophie had her character.

"Tell me about this betrothal of yours," Mrs. Twisden said. They all looked up as Mary brought a tray of tea and cakes in.

Sophie met his eyes, and he saw the twinkle of humor in her gaze. Let him answer this how he might. She had never told him whether or not she had admitted to the truth about their meeting or whether she had said they'd met in England.

"I believe it was love at first sight," he said, seeking Sophie's eyes once again. When their eyes met, something in his chest expanded. It was a moment before he pulled his regard away. "It has not been a long acquaintance—I am sure you must know that. But I could see at once that Sophie was a remarkable woman."

Now his eyes were fully on the elderly Mrs. Twisden as he elaborated on his supposed fiancée's qualities—a fiancée who somehow felt more fitted to the role the longer he spoke. "She is courageous and quick-thinking. She speaks French beautifully, and I can easily picture her leading society from our drawing room. I shall not allow myself to be carried away with talk of her beauty, but leave that for her ears alone."

Sophie poured tea for her grandmother and then for him. When she handed the cup to him, he saw a slight wobble to her fingers, and he sought her eyes again, but she evaded his look. There was heightened color in her cheeks.

His words had been too strong—he had suspected as much. And what was he doing? He had not planned on saying any of that when he'd arrived in the sitting room. He had been trying to reassure her grandmother, and thus support Sophie. Instead, he made theirs sound as though it were the greatest love match of the century. He sipped his tea, which was too hot, and set the cup down abruptly. The urbane manners he had perfected were nowhere to be found.

"So you both plan to live in France, I suppose," Mrs. Twisden said. "It makes sense. You cannot easily be a marquis and care for your land from England."

Sophie remained obstinately silent, and he could guess the reason. It was up to him to carry the conversation since he had plunged them into this imbroglio. "Do you mind it?"

Mrs. Twisden had not picked up her tea, and he wondered if she had the strength to do so. He remembered Sophie's request that he not overstay his welcome.

"I do not. I spent many good years in Paris. I think she will be quite happy here." She looked up at him with an endearing mixture of pleading and mischief. "I only wonder if you would have room in your house for an old woman?"

Sophie looked at him now, her eyes wide with alarm. This engagement would take on a frightening proportion were he to promise her grandmother she might reside with him. That was an obligation from which he could not easily extricate himself—not without being a cur.

"I do not know of any old woman," he said, smiling, "only one who has retained all her charm." Flattery yes, but also stalling for time. "But I can promise you that anywhere Sophie is, her grandmother will be welcome."

There. He had answered without an outright falsehood, nor an outright promise. His eyes sought out Sophie's, wondering if she was satisfied with his response. She smiled. She was satisfied. But then, she broke his gaze rather quickly and dropped hers to her teacup. So perhaps not so satisfied.

It was all rather impossible, wasn't it? How to disentangle oneself from such a mess?

CHAPTER 14

After Basile intimated he would be taking his leave, Sophie said she would walk him to the door with an irrational desire to prolong their time together. She wished she could sit outside with him in the garden—for the day was warm but not overly hot, and there was a gentle breeze. But that would be a piece of folly. It was imperative she think rationally, especially when they seemed to be falling more deeply into their farce with time. Feelings would only complicate the matter. And yet, whenever she sat beside him, her reason seemed to evaporate like her breath in his nearness. It was as though the very particles of air that flew around them ceased in their orbit.

And never mind that when he spoke such flattering words, she could no longer remember that they had decided to pretend their engagement to the world at large. A small part of her wondered—couldn't help but wonder—if he'd meant anything of what he said. His words sounded so sincere, and she didn't take him for a liar.

These thoughts raced through her mind as she led him those few steps to the corridor and then the front door. She waved Mary away and opened the door herself. Instead of leaving, Basile paused at the threshold.

"That was more difficult than I thought it would be, but I believe we pulled through it rather well, don't you?" Basile said.

What did he expect her to say? How could she tell her grandmother now that she would not be marrying him? Mrs. Twisden had invited herself to live with him! Sophie knew her grandmother had her own house and enough of an income to keep herself with a small degree of comfort. But perhaps the life she had so long been used to was nothing to what she would have if she moved back to Paris and lived in the style of a marquis. This life was more in line with what she'd had when she was young before marrying Sophie's grandfather. Ah, but it was complicated.

"Sophie?" Basile prodded when she didn't reply.

"Yes." She stared at him, still thinking, still lost. "Yes, I think you handled that well."

He remained in place, his eyes searching hers. "I hope you will join me at the opera this week?" When she was silent still, he added, "It would be good for us to be seen together, for I have it on good authority that some of the queen's courtiers will be there, and I believe they will wish to regale her with interesting news. It seems you and I are the diversion of the moment."

His tone was light, but she could not match it and merely nodded. "I will join you there."

After another moment's hesitation, Basile took leave of her, and Sophie returned to the drawing room to help her grandmother. Jeannot had come in from the garden where she had been cutting herbs, expressing that she was sorry to have missed the marquis as she helped Mrs. Twisden to her feet.

"Grandmama, will you rest now?"

Her grandmother spared only a brief smile, for she appeared to have grown fatigued from the short visit. As Jeannot supported her arm, she stopped and lifted her hand to pat Sophie's cheek.

"The marquis appears to be deeply in love with you, my dear. I cannot tell you how glad that makes me. I am determined to be well so I may assist in the wedding preparations." She then continued to her room without waiting for an answer, which was fortunate because Sophie had none.

Basile, in love with me? That couldn't be. How had she gotten herself into such a jumble of lies? Mary collected the tea tray and was passing by with it. At once, Sophie needed to leave the house or she would end up pacing the garden, and it was too small to hold her frustration.

"Mary, would you be able to accompany me again to the Tuileries? I wish to walk there."

"Of course," the maid answered. "I will put these away and be right with you." Mary hurried into the kitchen and was heard to be washing the tea cups and saucers and placing them on their shelf.

Sophie regretted pulling Mary away from her other work, but she could not walk alone any more than she could stay here. She hoped Mary would understand her need for silence.

When they entered the Tuileries some twenty minutes later, Sophie at a nice brisk walk that Mary had no trouble keeping up with, she began to feel better. Mary was indeed understanding of her need for silence and left Sophie to her thoughts as she tried to sort through her tangle of feelings. She should blame Basile, she supposed. And she would—except that she enjoyed spending time with him and hated to think what would have happened if they'd never met.

She would be going to parties where she knew no one. Or, *no*! She would be home nursing her grandmother with Sheldon coming by every day to add irritation to misery. She could only be grateful for the direction her stay in Paris had taken.

But then, it was becoming increasingly difficult to think through how they were to manage the end to their sham betrothal. She liked him very well—*all too well*, if she were going to be honest with herself. But she did not want to marry a man who had not courted her in earnest. A man who played the part convincingly but did not truly love her.

They rounded the large pond with a fountain placed in its center. On the side of the rounded path, marble statues were placed in between the leafy branches of trees and looked down upon her from their pedestals. The trickling of water in the fountain soothed.

A gentleman headed in her direction. As they were about to cross paths, he lifted his head and paused. "Miss Twisden?"

Sophie stopped as recognition dawned. "Mr. Arlington. A pleasure to meet you here." She pulled her thoughts from the place that had no answers and focused on her countryman. "Do you walk here often?"

"I have started to of late. I like to come here to think." Although a smile accompanied his words, it looked pained. She wondered if Zoé had anything to do with his unhappy look. "Would you like to walk with me a ways?" he asked.

Sophie nodded and turned in his direction as Mary followed at a distance.

"I must congratulate you on your betrothal," he said. "It seems you will be remaining in France on a more permanent basis, will you not?"

It was Sophie's turn to look pained. Another opportunity to lie, and she found she did not want to. But she couldn't give up the act when they were working so hard to make it convincing. "I...believe that is the plan. It's too early to tell."

He peered at her more closely, his unpowdered dark hair catching the sun in its golden reflection. He was a handsome man, but his eyes seemed dull when compared to *another* set of eyes and his mouth was absent of the humor that revealed a quick wit.

"Is there trouble in your engagement?" As soon he had spoken the words, he warded off the imagined rebuke with his hands. "I do not mean to pry, but I couldn't help but think that perhaps you are not sure of your choice, and that explains your hesitation."

They walked on as Sophie thought how best to answer. "There is a bit of trouble between us, but I hope nothing too serious. I hope we may sort it out."

There! Let him make of that what he would. Perhaps it would make the eventual end to their betrothal more believable if she were to hint now at some discord.

He continued to walk, lost in thought as he touched his cane to the ground with every other footstep. He wore the colors of court mourning, and the shades of gray did nothing to make him appear more lively. "I can certainly understand such a thing. When you attempt a love match with a woman—rather, with *a person* from a different culture, it is sure to raise misunderstandings. And sometimes those seem insurmountable. Perhaps they are."

Sophie glanced at him, and when he didn't elaborate, she said, "Forgive me for my impertinence, but I believe you have developed a friendship with Mademoiselle Sainte-Croix?"

He tossed her a look, his expression sober as he turned

to face forward. "I won't pretend to misunderstand you, for it must be very obvious. I believe she has let you into her confidence?" Sophie nodded, and he went on. "I thought once that we might have a great partiality for each other, but I am beginning to fear I was wrong. I am coming to believe she has not even a heart to give away."

Sophie walked on, tempted to urge him to be more extravagant in his pursuit, but holding herself back. What if she really did not know Zoé as she thought she did, and she encouraged Mr. Arlington to pursue her, only then to give him true cause for a broken heart? Sophie reflected on the wisest course of action for only a minute before deciding she couldn't stay completely silent when she thought Zoé might be suffering too.

"I do know Mademoiselle Sainte-Croix a very little bit. And although I cannot know her well enough to speak with any sort of certainty, I will tell you what I have noticed. When she is with you, her face is alive. When she thinks you are looking, she is animated. But when you seem disapproving and move away, her expression grows dull."

He lifted his head, as though the thought ballooned him with hope. "I should very much like to believe you."

Sophie smiled and kept her eyes trained ahead. "I can only tell you what I've observed. From what I've heard her say, I cannot be convinced that her heart is completely untouched. And she does have a heart to give away, I believe," she added, "for she accompanied Basile to my house to see how my grandmother fared. Then she returned to escort me to a soirée so I might have a chance for diversion during my stay in Paris. That is not the act of a woman who has no heart to give."

Mr. Arlington breathed in deeply and glanced at her. "I suppose I might try again."

"I suppose you might," Sophie said, returning his smile. They both stopped and faced each other.

"I regret leaving you, but do you mind...?"

Sophie shook her head. "My maid is with me, and I wish to walk a little longer."

"Very well, Miss Twisden." He held out his hand and she placed hers in it.

"Mr. Arlington."

They parted ways in a most amicable manner, and she hoped she might have helped him—and Zoé—to find their way through the intricacies of a courtship between two people who were as different as they were.

Now, if only someone would help her with her own.

The night of the opera, Sophie was dressed and waiting by the time Basile came for her. She was also resolved, having decided to do what was needed to keep up the appearances of a true betrothal while keeping her heart firmly intact. These past few days, she had lost her way, walking around like a lovesick girl, but now it was time to use the situation to her full advantage.

For it was advantageous to be engaged to a marquis, even if it was one she had no intention of marrying. It would give her status in Paris while she was here. And as much as it chafed, she had to admit she preferred to be under his mercy than Sheldon's. He would see to it that she and her grandmother were safely returned to England and would not expect marriage as payment. That was an improvement.

Never mind that you wouldn't exactly deplore being married to him, a small voice inside whispered.

But that was neither here nor there. Sheldon had to be utterly convinced she was out of his grasp until she was no longer under his mercy. When she was back in England, she could pursue her own life and disappear completely from his view. Such a thing was hardly possible while living next door to him. And she would find a way to pay both him and Basile back for any bills incurred on her behalf. She would have to! Forget a simple country life in the dower house that was hers. She would have to rent out her house and find a paid position in addition to supplement her small income in order to pay him back.

These were the rational thoughts she forced to parade through her mind as she readied herself for the evening. Jeannot had come to her aid once again with her coiffure. It was lovely, really, the way her features improved when there was height in the back with the *boucles* on the sides and the long curl placed artfully over her shoulder—the curl that Basile had toyed with and left her nearly faint.

So when the knock sounded on the door, Sophie was already standing in the corridor, giving a final adjustment to the laces over her gray stomacher. Her French corset cinched her waist in neatly and gave a beautifully feminine form with her paniers on either side adding volume. She had placed her own patch onto a powdered face. In Paris, she was learning of the necessity to appear modish. It would be better to go about *en nature* than to be considered sadly out of fashion.

The sight of Basile entering caused her breath to catch. He was still wearing the sober colors of court mourning, but his coat was embroidered with silver. And the silver hair powder he wore in complement stood in stark contrast to his dark blue eyes and the general strength in his features and bearing. He swept off his hat, extended his leg and bowed low.

"Behold in me, your eternal admirer," he said, smiling.

Jeannot came into the corridor then and admonished him in familiar French to take proper care of Mademoiselle Sophie and see that she returned home without being overly fatigued.

Sophie smiled at her and turned to Basile, saying in English, "You needn't waste your compliments on me when there is no one here to see."

He leaned down to kiss Jeannot on the cheek, which she found charming in its familiarity, then turned to her. "Truth is never wasted. Are you ready?"

Sophie nodded and they went outdoors to his carriage. She had forgotten to ask him but quite thought Zoé and her family might be accompanying them that evening. After all, it was not as though they needed to talk about flirtation and coordinate their behavior toward one another as they had the last time. But the carriage was empty when he helped her into it.

Basile snapped the door shut and tapped on the roof with his cane as the horses darted forward.

"Who are we to sit with today?" Sophie asked him.

"We shall be in my opera box, and I've invited the Sainte-Croix family to join us there. I hope this meets with your approval?" He raised an eyebrow.

She tossed one of her shoulders. "Of course."

It was odd. He was being flirtatious but was somehow colder than usual, and it troubled her. Perhaps he regretted everything—the engagement which she reminded herself was his own fault—the flirting, the stack of her bills. His reserve certainly seemed to indicate regret.

How had their lives become so entwined? For heaven's sake, even his former nurse was residing at her house and caring for her grandmother. And he was in receipt of the entirety of her bills—Sheldon's brief note told her as much. It was mortifying! She would have to find some way to pull back herself, to salvage her dignity.

They spoke little on the way to the opera, and when they arrived, she allowed him to help her out of the carriage as she stared up at the vast stone façade of the opera house. They followed the streams of people inside, and Sophie lifted her wide skirt as she navigated the stairs. When they arrived inside and were in the broad corridor, Sophie stopped dead in her tracks. There, on the other end of the hall talking to Sheldon, was Mrs. Betteridge. Sophie's blood drained from her face. Her, of all people, here in France? That would destroy everything!

"Oh dear." She lay a suddenly cold hand on Basile's arm.

"*Qu'est-ce qu'il y a?*" Basile looked down at her hand, then back up, catching sight of her expression. "Sophie, what is it?"

For a moment she was silent. It felt like the floor was falling in as her mind reeled. "Mrs. Betteridge has come to Paris."

Basile continued to regard her, clearly unenlightened by her words, so she elaborated. "She is the woman who supposedly introduced us at the *al fresco* picnic in London, and now Sheldon is learning directly from her lips that she has no idea who you are."

CHAPTER 15

Basile stared ahead at the disaster unfolding before him. *Mais non—fichtre!* The meeting they claimed to have had in London was about to be proven false, and the queen would surely find *that* piece out. He quickly tempered his alarm. It was merely a challenge. They would rise to it.

"Trust me, Sophie," he murmured as the peacock moved forward with the Englishwoman of indeterminate age at his side.

"Sophie," Mr. Cholmsley said. "*Moe-syur,*" he added with a cold bow toward Basile. "I believe you know our friend, Mrs. Betteridge?"

"I have not had that pleasure," Basile said, bowing.

Cholmsley's brows rose as though he were surprised by the admission. What did he expect? Basile could hardly pretend to the falsehood now that the woman was standing before them.

"Sophie, you said you had met the marquis at Mrs. Betteridge's *al fresco* picnic. Was it not so?"

"Mrs. Betteridge, how do you do?" Sophie asked. "I hope your journey was pleasant. When did you arrive?"

"Why, only on Wednesday. But is this not the oddest thing? Could it be true that you met your *fiancé* at my picnic? I don't have any recollection of having met him, much less having invited him."

"No, no. There is some misunderstanding which can surely be explained." Sophie's expression was once again veiled, although there was a tinge of color on her cheeks. "Might I introduce you to Monsieur Gervain, Marquis de Verdelle? He is indeed my *fiancé*."

"But you said—" Sheldon moved forward to stand over Sophie, and Basile gave her a light tug so that he could take her place in front of the peacock.

"I believe you have misunderstood the lady, for I am meeting the charming Mrs. Betteridge for the first time today." Basile stared at the Englishman pointedly.

M. Cholmsley peered around him at Sophie. "Did you meet this man for the first time in Paris? I cannot imagine when you would have had time." A thought occurred to him. "Did you meet him for the first time on that *day*?"

"It's the oddest thing," Mrs. Betteridge repeated, clearly lost as she looked from one to the other for a sensible explanation. She did not give the impression of possessing a sensible thought of her own.

"This hardly matters, Sheldon. What matters is that Basile and I are to be married." Sophie looked up as a bell sounded somewhere in the distance. "And the opera is about to begin. If you will excuse us?"

She began to walk forward and turned only to say, "I hope you will have a lovely stay in Paris, Mrs. Betteridge. I am sure we will meet at one of the ambassador's events."

Basile moved to take her arm and escort her to his box

seat. Earlier that day, something had put him in a bad temper, irritating him like a small pebble in his boot, except he could not sort out what it was. He had come to the decision it was time to maintain a more respectful distance—something more in line with what two people who were only pretending to be engaged should be displaying. His first glimpse of Sophie in another stylish gown and French coiffure that evening threatened to unravel those plans, for he found himself admiring her more than he should.

It was a dangerous game to play, and he was seeing now just to what extent. To act as though one were betrothed in earnest when one had no intention of seeing it through. To flirt and openly admire and caress cheeks and shoulders of a gently born maiden when one was determined to remain in the bachelor state for some years to come—this was something that should not be undertaken lightly. He had seen firsthand how dangerous it was when he had practically needed to leap away from her at the last soirée to keep from allowing his attraction and admiration to lead him into forbidden territory.

She was walking quickly at his side, and the corridors were growing thin of crowds.

"I am beginning to feel we have made a grave mistake," Sophie said breathlessly before stopping to look at him. "Do you not feel it?"

Basile furrowed his brows. "Why? Because part of the story we told can be proven as untrue? I don't see why that is the problem you say it is. The main thing is that we have both escaped unwanted attention."

She remained in place, despite the sounds reaching them of the comedy beginning to unfold on stage. "Have we, though? I fear we have only plunged ourselves deeper into unwanted attention. Mrs. Betteridge's arrival in Paris will lead Sheldon to spread the news near and far that we have lied about at least part of our engagement. I am sure it is only time before Madame Bordenave will herald it as well."

"That does not matter. I know how society functions, and the thing to do now is to double down and prove that we are indeed a love match, whether it is of long date or a *coup de foudre* on the streets of Paris." As he studied her, he felt her withdraw from him, sensed her fears. Rather than running while he could, everything in him wanted to convince her not to give way to those fears. Perhaps it really had been love at first sight. If that was so, he really should run.

She paused and searched his eyes intently. "But why take it further?" She broke his gaze. "I mean, clearly we cannot announce that we have pulled the wool over everyone's eyes and that it is a farce. But why go so far as to pretend we are madly in love?"

He held out his hand, and she slipped hers into it. There was that trust again. "Because we will never have anyone convinced if we do not play the part well. And we must play the part, for—as you have said—no one can know we have begun all this as a prank. Our only choice is to play it out until the end as we have decided. It is ours to direct as we will."

She met his eyes again, and he could not read her expression, but her look of doubt seemed to give way to one of resolve. And with it, a frost that had not been there before.

"Very well. If that is what is required, let us do our very best." She turned to walk into the box. Basile followed behind, struggling to think how he might convince her that all would be well when he could not quite see his own way through.

His family box contained six seats. Madame Sainte-Croix and Jeanne were sitting in the seats closest to the railing, and Charles was seated in the middle row beside Zoé. Basile hadn't told her that he had invited her swain, but he could tell from her upright posture that she was more conscious of Charles's presence than what was occurring on stage. If Charles couldn't win her hand with such gifts as a darkened opera house and three hours with which to woo a woman at his disposal, then he didn't deserve to win her.

Sophie sat in the last row, shaded by the overhead curtain. Basile took the seat next to her, glancing around the boxes on the opposite side of the theater. More than one person caught his regard and nodded in acknowledgment. One of them was the Comte de Vaudreuil, who was known to be a particular favorite of the queen. He was watching Basile closely.

Basile leaned in to Sophie and caught the bergamot and clove scent of her powder. Her coiffure was really done in such a charming manner thanks to Jeannot—their nurse had often helped Basile's sister when the maids were too busy. Sophie had put on her own patch that day, higher up on her cheek and it was near enough to tempt him to touch it. He remained in this position of contemplation long enough that he felt Sophie freeze at his side.

"What is it?" she whispered. "You are staring at me."

So much for his resolve to act in a more distant manner. He could not resist the pull to flirt with her. "'Tis only that I spotted the Comte de Vaudreuil, and I am giving him a show so he can report back to the queen."

"Ah."

The word was spoken lightly and after a moment, she relaxed into him, allowing her arm to sink into his. His heart skittered out of his chest and applauded with the rest of the audience as the comedy below came to an end. Slowly she turned her face to his until their eyes were level and she was staring into his soul. "Perhaps we should give him a show. The earl and anyone else who might be watching."

She turned her eyes forward, and having that forthright gaze withdrawn left him reeling. Then, before he could collect his wits, she brought her left hand over and skimmed her hand along his coat sleeve. Slowly, she traced her fingers down the length of his arm until she had reached his bare hand. He swallowed.

"This is a fine coat. So unlike our English ones. Simple, and no lace dripping from the sleeves. How do you call this in French?"

"It's a *justaucorp*." His voice was thready, which only served to irritate him. He was the one who was supposed to be flirting.

"*Just-au-corp*. I see. It hugs the body, is that it? I did not know this word." The touch of her fingers was back, trailing a line down his sleeve, but this time he grabbed her hand and held it in a viselike grip.

"Mademoiselle Twisden, what are you doing?"

She turned wide, innocent eyes to him—eyes that held a glint nonetheless—before she leaned in to murmur, "Why, I am only assisting you in your performance, Monsieur le Marquis. We have Madame Bordenave, Mr. Cholmsley, and Mrs. Betteridge to convince, and now apparently the queen, as well. If all the flirtation comes from you, how can anyone know if your mad passion is returned?"

He set his mouth in a thin line. "I do not believe you

need to do more than receive my overt displays of affection."

"Oh." Her mouth formed a perfect circle, puckering a set of pink, luscious lips as her eyes came to rest on his mouth, but she did not move away. Instead she batted her eyelashes once and lifted her eyes to his. "Are you uncomfortable being on the receiving end of my overtures when it is all merely a farce?"

She kept her face close, her eyes never leaving his. Around them, the second act had begun, which was the tragic opera. The singers' voices filled the theater and seemed to vibrate even within him. Tucked back in the shadows of the box, he had the sensation of being shrouded from the rest of the opera-goers. They were in a world of their own making. In front of them, Charles leaned in to whisper in Zoé's ear, and in front, Madame Sainte-Croix and her daughter both listened to the opera in apparent rapture. Basile slipped the fan from Sophie's grasp and opened it fully to shield them from the audience. He then leaned in and saw a jolt of shock in the gleam of her eyes as he closed the distance between them.

He had meant to tease, had meant to give her a taste of her own medicine. But now that he had drawn so near to her, he wanted nothing more than to kiss her. The pull was too potent to resist, and he touched his lips to hers. She froze.

He intended to do no more, but when she still had not moved, he became filled with the awareness of her scent and the softness of her lips as the sounds of *Orphée et Euridice* enveloped them in the booming melody of Gluck's tragic opera. So, he did more than just touch her lips. He kissed her. Then he felt her come to life and lost himself in the sensation of her kissing him back.

"Euridice—" The castrato's voice rang out above the choir, and Basile's head spun as his center of gravity seemed to fall away.

He pulled back, and Sophie ducked her head, retiring into her seat and bringing a draft of cold air where she had been. His head buzzed, his heart still pounding from the forbidden taste of her lips. He should not have done that, should not have given into the temptation.

Basile snapped her fan shut and handed it back to her, then rubbed his chin in his hand. Only then did he gather the courage to look up at the audience to see if they had been observed. He had not intended to kiss her. That was going beyond flirtation. It would provide more proof than they needed to validate their engagement—more than was wanted, for it would be hard to pull back from.

Sophie's head was still down, but Basile glanced around the opera and saw the satisfied expression of de Vaudreuil and the furious expression of Cholmsley.

Parbleu! The queen would surely hear of it now.

CHAPTER 16

Sophie sat on the stone bench in the garden, immobile, removed from her surroundings, reliving every minute of what had transpired at the opera the night before. She thought about her sudden decision to flirt with Basile the way he had done with her. It had certainly been a bold move. She had wanted to prove a point to the marquis, had wanted him to feel a fraction of what she felt when he touched her in such a way or placed the weight of his regard on her. And he *had* felt it as she had, of that she was sure, for it had led him to kiss her. When her mind came to rest on the moment his lips pressed onto hers, time came to a standstill. He would never have done that if she hadn't flirted. Despite that, she could not be sorry.

"Your grandmother is much improved." Jeannot had come to find her in the garden. Sophie had not heard her approach. "She is reading in the sitting room and did not even need a rest after lunch."

"It is good news." The weight of Sophie's thoughts made casual speech difficult.

The nurse busied herself, pulling some errant weeds and cutting stems of thyme that she had been using to make *tisanes* for Mrs. Twisden that helped with the cough.

"I think my presence is no longer *imperative*, mademoiselle," the nurse said. "I think tomorrow I will leave. It is good timing, *je l'avoue*, for Madame Thérèse is coming from Tours before her confinement makes such a visit impossible. I will go see to her."

"Yes, of course," Sophie said, pulled at last out of her reverie by the news. They had been lucky to have the nurse for as long as they had. Sophie stood and took Jeannot's strong hand in hers. "I do not know how I can thank you for your kindness to us."

The nurse patted Sophie's arm with the strength of someone much younger. "*C'est naturel.* Until I am called upon to care for your *enfant* with the marquis, I was happy to be otherwise employed."

The nurse turned to walk back toward the house when her words penetrated. *Her* infant? Her baby with the marquis?

"Jeannot," she called out before stopping short. How could she explain that there would never be an *enfant*? She had avoided telling Mary about the engagement, although the maid must surely know. But Sophie did not wish to see the nurse disappointed when nothing came of it. "Do you... do you know about the engagement?"

"Why, of course!" the nurse said, turning back with a smile that made her appear even more youthful. "Your grandmother could not keep such news to herself and knew she would have a sympathetic ear in me. Although why Basile did not tell me himself... I will have to scold him on the matter."

"Yes, do that," Sophie muttered as soon as the nurse

had walked away. She would like to see Basile try to explain the situation to his beloved nurse.

She went inside and down the cool, dim corridor. As she stared at the door to the sitting room, she put her hands on her waist, readying herself to enter it. This was becoming ever more complicated. She would take her grandmother into her confidence, but the truth would only cause her to worry about their debt to Sheldon. Or worse—cause Sophie's grandmother to try to throw her back into his path.

And then there was the odd feeling she couldn't explain to herself that the betrothal was actually real. Or that she wished it were real. The thought caused a heaviness to settle in her chest. She could never admit such a thing to Basile who—for all he was a kind and considerate man underneath his playful exterior—would be appalled to think she was tempted even a little bit to hold him to his proposal.

She would not, no matter how much it cost her. And the lead weight that had taken up residence inside of her showed her just how much it did cost her.

In the drawing room, her grandmother sat reading a book with a cup of tea beside her. She lifted her head and smiled. "My dear Sophie. As you can see, I am very much more myself. I believe your good news is what brought about such a swift recovery."

"I am so pleased," Sophie said, feeling entirely wretched.

"It is time we begin to think about your engagement dinner. It will be expected for someone like the marquis. I must apply my mind to how we might arrange it properly." She sipped her tea then lifted her head, applying herself to how they might throw an elaborate meal with scarcely a farthing to their name.

"Grandmama, I fear we do not have the means for an engagement dinner—" Sophie began.

A knock on the door cut her off, and she heard Mary hurrying down the corridor to answer it. There was the sound of an unknown voice—a messenger, it seemed, delivering something to the maid. The front door closed and Mary appeared in the sitting room.

"This came for you, miss."

She handed her a letter and Sophie studied the mark imprinted on the deep red wax that sealed the paper. The imprint contained two shields, one with three *fleur-de-lys* and the other whose detail was more difficult to make out, but which seemed to have a lion and a sword. Above the shields, a crown was easily distinguishable and that gave her the first clue. Her heart began to thud. With trembling fingers, she opened the missive, for that must be what this was.

Indeed. 'Twas a summons.

Chère Mlle Sophie Twisden, the letter began. Her eyes rapidly skimmed its contents. The queen wished for the pleasure of her company on the 11th of August, Thursday next, to partake of a *repas de fiançailles* to celebrate her betrothal to M. Basile Thomas Hortense Gervain, le Marquis de Verdelle, etc. Her grandmother was also invited, showing how knowledgeable the queen was of their situation. The address given was to the Petit Trianon in Versailles.

Sophie looked up, first with alarm, then with a look of manufactured pleasure when she saw her grandmother's confusion. "'Tis an invitation to celebrate our engagement, given by the queen herself. We are invited for next Thursday to Versailles."

Her grandmother clasped her hands together. "Oh, oh, my dear! I simply cannot tell you how delighted I am for you. I could never have predicted you would make such an excellent match. If I had, I never would have pressed you to consider Sheldon's advances."

The news brought Mrs. Twisden to her feet, and she would not be deterred when Sophie tried to lead her back to her chair. "No, no, I am perfectly well now," she said. "And I will surely be well enough to attend by next Thursday. It is a most fortunate thing I had a dress made in gray silk damask before setting out for France, though I little knew how I would need it."

She continued along in that vein while Sophie's mind reeled. She needed to speak with Basile, but did not feel she could apply to him directly since they weren't actually engaged. It did not matter that she had been bold in her behavior toward him. She knew her limits. Would he come to guide her on the matter of the invitation? Surely he would have received his own? It seemed too much for her to wait for him to call.

Returning vague replies to her grandmother's questions and observations, Sophie formed a plan to visit Zoé rather than sit and wait for the marquis to call at his leisure. For she could not delay her response and needed to know what to do. This engagement had taken on gargantuan proportions.

With such excitement, it was not long before her grandmother did need to rest, and Sophie was able to ask Mary to accompany her. They would soon be constrained once Jeannot was no longer there to care for her grandmother, for Mary could not be in two places at once.

The Sainte-Croix address was not so far they could not walk, so she set them out at a brisk pace. Please God that Zoé would be there. When they knocked at the entrance, the servant answered the door with the news that she was indeed at home.

Sophie was then shown into the drawing room, where Madame Sainte-Croix and her daughters sat talking to a visitor whose own daughter appeared to be the same age as Jeanne. As Sophie entered, Zoé was already on her feet. The introductions were performed, and Sophie curtsied to the guests.

"It is the first time you have come to visit," Zoé said. "Dare I hope it means your grandmother is doing well enough to leave her at home?"

"She is better," Sophie said, returning her smile. "She will continue to need rest, but I have every hope she will soon be able to accept invitations."

After a moment, in which Sophie tried to think how to gain a private audience, Zoé turned to her mother. "Would you excuse us, *Maman*? I would like to show Sophie our garden, for she has never seen it."

Her mother acquiesced then turned back to their guests, and Zoé led the way out of doors, grabbing a parasol that stood near the door. Their garden was much smaller than Sophie's, surprisingly, given how large the house was. But it was inviting with a neatly manicured lawn and carefully trimmed bushes, and even plots of flowers in colorful varieties. Zoé led her to a bubbling fountain placed in front of a bench whose arched trellis of clematis provided shade. They took a seat under it.

"I was wondering if you had news concerning your engagement and wished to be private," Zoé said. "I knew my mother wouldn't mind, for the Aborgasts are intimate friends."

Zoé had read her wishes correctly, but now that the private audience was given to her, Sophie found it hard to leap right into her purpose for coming. "Have you seen Mr. Arlington since the opera?" she said instead. It was rather intrusive as far as questions went, but the words were out.

Fortunately, Zoé did not seem to resent such familiarity. She did allow her lips to pull into a pout. "We are at odds again."

"Really? What happened? It seemed you were of perfect accord when we met at the opera." Despite herself, her curiosity for Mr. Arlington's prospects suddenly seemed more of a moment than her own.

Zoé used the tip of the parasol to gouge into the dirt at her feet. "We were, and perhaps I had hoped we might begin to see eye to eye, but now..." She trailed off and focused on the pattern she was creating at her feet.

"And now?" Sophie prodded.

"Now, I fear it is not to be. After you left, Le Comte de Vaudreuil came to find me and pulled me quite out of Charles's arm." She brought her stare to Sophie's as though compelled to explain. "He is such a flirt, you see, that one cannot resist him. One must laugh. Everyone knows he means nothing by it. I responded as any woman would do, to be sure. But Charles walked off and abandoned me there."

"Abandoned you? Do you mean you had come to the opera together?" Sophie knit her brows. It did not seem like him, though she could not claim to know him well.

"No. I came with my mother and sister, but he left with scarcely a by-your-leave. It enrages me, this off-hand leave-taking as though I were no more to him than a...a puppy. He clearly does not esteem me if he can do such a thing."

Sophie remembered how miserable he had looked when they'd met at the Tuileries. She had encouraged him to try again. "Perhaps," she said gently, "he fears you would rather be with the *comte* than with him."

"Then he doesn't consider me worth the fight. Or he is afraid to lose—and that is just as bad."

Sophie let her eyes drift as she inhaled the scents of the garden and worked at the problem in her mind. Should she stay clear of a situation that did not directly concern her? A situation in which she could not even be sure her advice would be useful or welcome? But then Mr. Arlington's face loomed before her, a picture of misery. And even Zoé's face was troubled when they were at odds. No, it was clear Sophie needed to say something.

"Perhaps it is not that he so little considers you or that he is afraid. From what I know of him, scant though that is, I believe it is rather because he is a gentleman and therefore will not press you. He naturally prefers to be assured of your partiality to him above all others. When he is sure of your regard, he will fight for you. That does not reveal cowardice or a lack of concern—it is simply good breeding. At least for an Englishman."

Zoé turned to study her, her expression contemplative. "You said something like this before. *Do* you think it's his gentlemanly ways that cause him to react thus?" A laugh escaped her. "I don't believe the French male has such a notion. He takes what he wants."

"Which would you rather have?" Sophie asked, a smile forming. She had not minded when Basile had stolen the kiss from her. Although it was hardly as though he had stolen it. She had handed it to him on a silver platter.

"Oh, I suppose I would rather be allowed to choose." After a silence which Sophie did not try to fill, Zoé exhaled. "Very well. I will show him my partiality—*even when* a most charming *comte* or other gentleman comes to flirt—for I have been quite miserable. We shall see if what you say is true."

"I think that is a very good notion," Sophie said, inwardly willing Mr. Arlington to do his part.

Zoé sat up straighter and turned a smiling countenance to her. "But then tell me how you are. How is your engagement?" She nudged her with her arm. "Is it becoming more real by the day?"

The question, said in jest, little helped. "On the contrary, it is becoming frighteningly hard to maintain such an imposture." Sophie slipped her hand into her pocket and pulled out the letter from the queen and handed it to Zoé, who opened it and perused the elegant scrawl.

"*Ciel!*"

Heavens was right! "I can only suppose Basile received something similar. How are we to keep this up when the queen has taken notice of it?"

Zoé read it twice then set it on her lap, allowing a soft, "How I wish I could go," to escape before she sat upright. "But this is not about me."

"What am I to *do*?" Sophie asked her. "Basile does not seem at all concerned over the entanglement we have gotten ourselves into."

"Basile possesses a maddening ability to do whatever he wishes without sparing a thought for how inconvenient others might find it," Zoé replied tartly. When Sophie pressed her hands to her eyes, she touched her arm. "No, I should not have said that. Though he is not considerate like

Charles is, he does have a remarkable way of seeing things through."

"I know she is not *my* queen, but Marie-Antoinette is still a queen. Do I lie to her?" Sophie turned to face Zoé, desperate for comfort, for guidance.

"I think only Basile can truly answer that question, and we shall have to apply to him for what to do." Zoé handed the letter back to Sophie. "His sister should have arrived in Paris by now. I believe she was to have come yesterday. That will give me a reason to visit him and find out what he means to do."

She patted Sophie's arm. "You may trust him to keep you from all harm, or I shall have something to say to him."

CHAPTER 17

Basile sat at *Le Gradot* with an untouched cup of coffee in front of him. He had gone to the café for distraction, but now that he sat here...*imprisoned* by the memories of his kiss with Sophie—memories that somehow seemed physically weighted—he wished only to remain in the enthrallment of those memories rather than seeking the distraction he had come for.

Noises erupted around him as the café's occupants called for a beer or coffee, a pastry, or a dish of sorbet. Basile had taken his breakfast earlier that morning without tasting anything and even now could not stomach the thought of anything but coffee, which sat in front of him growing cold. A waiter approached with a newspaper, but he waved him away.

What had Sophie been about last night, flirting with him in such a direct manner? It placed him in a difficult, almost vulnerable position, because for once he was not in command. She should know what such flirtation led to—it paralyzed a man, or it set him on fire. For him, it had done both. He was first paralyzed under her touch. That was, until he had kissed her and became consumed with a fire that incinerated his reason.

His thoughts took him hostage in pleasant agony as he grappled with the question of why she had instigated that particular act of spellbinding. He supposed the secret lay in her words: that in order for their charade to be believable, she had to flirt back with him. But he also wondered if she did so out of retaliation, wishing to show him what it felt like when he did the same to her. He knew she stilled under his touch. Knew it affected her.

No one had come to distract him or disturb his peace in his hour at the café, so Basile stood to pay his shot. It was time he went home anyway. His sister and her husband were supposed to come and stay at the marquis's family home for the length of her confinement. It was not that her husband did not have his own house in Paris, but Thérèse wished to be surrounded by all that was familiar, she had said.

Basile exited the café and turned left onto the Quai de l'Ecole to walk the short distance to the Pont Neuf, still troubled in his mind. No woman had ever disturbed him in the way Sophie did. That he would be tempted to pretend a friendship where there had been none might be explained away by his own whimsy and mischief, but to send his nurse to assist her within a week's acquaintance? Or that he would look forward to seeing her and discussing anything from his feelings on being the marquis to the art of flirting —that he would announce a betrothal without actually contracting one! His behavior was nothing short of inexplicable.

Did he indeed wish to marry her?

The foreign thought stopped him dead in his tracks. That caused a tradesman walking behind him to bump into him, first with an oath, then a mumbled pardon delivered with a lowered brow.

"*C'est moi*," Basile murmured in return. No, no, no. It could not be. He was too young to be thinking of marriage. He intended to wait until he was forty at the very least before making such an attempt. If one was going to throw away years of one's life, then better to do so when the very best were at least behind him. He could enter the state of matrimony when his youth was a thing of the past.

He crossed the bridge, hardly noticing the Seine rushing beneath. The moving water brought a cooling breeze to temper the August heat. He lifted his gaze ahead to the even row of cream-colored stone houses on the opposite quay.

Would it really be throwing his best years away in being married to her, though? Sophie never bored him. By turns she amused him, enchanted him, and touched him with her strength—that and by her dependence on him, when he suspected she was unused to being vulnerable. She trusted him, which was a novel experience outside a few close friendships. As he was the Gervain family's very last hope for the marquisate's lineage, he had not often met with such blind trust. Instead, his parents had considered him something of a profligate, which was not very fair, since he generally spent his funds on travel.

By the time he arrived at his gate, he was no closer to knowing whether he wished to be wed in earnest or not. The servant opened the iron gate to admit him, and ahead, he saw his brother-in-law accompanying the groom to the stables. So, his sister had arrived.

And there she was, walking along the garden path toward his house, arm in arm with Zoé. A flash of irritation seized him. His sister he could manage, but Zoé? She knew about his betrothal, and nothing would astonish him more than if she managed to keep that information to herself. He did not wish to discuss it before he had carefully sorted through his intentions.

At the sound of his approaching footsteps, the women turned arm in arm. Basile removed his hat, bowing to Zoé and kissing his sister. "*Bonjour*, Thérèse. I hope you have had a good journey."

"'Twas *agréable*." She turned to Zoé, adding, "You need not leave on my account. I require only a little tea to be restored to perfect health."

Zoé smiled at her, then turned to Basile. "I had not realized Thérèse was arriving only today or I should not have disturbed you. However, now that I am here, can you spare me a few minutes of your time?"

His hesitation lasted only a second. He would use it to tell her to keep silent on the subject of marriage. "Very well. Please, *entrez*," he said, leading the way indoors.

Zoé did not come to the point of her visit right away but engaged Thérèse in all manner of talk about the current mourning fashion in Paris, the scene of the Ranelagh ball, interspersing that with questions about her home in Tours. Thérèse's husband, Achille Lacaze, was a landed gentleman and a follower of Dupuy-Demporte's book, the *Gentleman Cultivator*, where he attempted to increase his profits through agriculture, much in the way the English did. Basile had never thought his sister would fit into such a bucolic lifestyle, but he had to own she seemed perfectly happy.

"You may say your piece in front of me if you wish, Zoé," Thérèse said at last. "I am not at all fatigued. I may even serve as chaperone."

Zoé's smile seemed to dim for a brief instant, but Basile was sure only he noticed it. "Wonderful," she replied.

She continued on with more innocent chatter while a servant brought refreshments, and Basile resigned himself to the inevitable, whatever that might be. A lengthy discussion that little interested him? Allusions to his farce that would only make him uncomfortable? Without Zoé, he could sort out how and what to tell his sister—this, and in his own timing.

"What do you think of Basile's engagement?" Zoé asked, cutting through a brief silence. Her eyes brimmed above her cup.

Basile coughed and spit some of his tea back in his cup as Thérèse turned to him. There was a short, stunned silence, then—

"*Impossible!*" Her eyes opened wide with the shock of it. "You—engaged? You must be joking."

Instead of answering her, he turned to Zoé. "I haven't exactly had time to speak of it, given that she has only just arrived. Perhaps you wish to come to the point of why you have called?" he added dangerously. He could throttle her.

"I was wondering if you had received the invitation from the queen for the *repas de fiançailles* she wishes to throw for you." Zoé smiled at him, seeming to enjoy his discomfort.

Basile's mouth dropped open and he was bereft of speech for nearly a full minute. The queen wished to take a hand in his engagement? That was disastrous! He stood and rang a bell for a servant. "Bring me my *courrier* at once," he told him.

"*Oui, monsieur.*"

"Who is this woman that has caught your fancy?" Thérèse asked. "I can scarcely believe you have decided to settle down. I have been waiting for it for an age! But why did you not write of it?"

It was foolish, perhaps, but Basile had hoped to avoid telling his sister at all, considering it was not a true betrothal. Zoé must have known it because she smirked at him over her cup.

The servant hurried back into the drawing room with a small pile of correspondence in hand, and Basile reached out for it as he decided on a reply. "I wished to tell you in person, of course."

His mood soured at the lie. He did not like telling falsehoods to his sister, but strangely nor did he wish to rush and tell her the betrothal was not real. She would have to find out when it was announced that he and Sophie had parted ways. She would have to learn of it as the queen did...

Basile pulled out a letter with a royal seal, his heart sinking. The words in it were clear. This was nothing short of a command—*that* could be read between the lines. The queen was looking for an excuse to inaugurate the Petit Trianon as her own, now that the former king's mistress and her rival, Madame Du Barry, had been sent away. She was also probably hoping to relieve the tedium of the court mourning through a private party.

"Well?" Basile prompted Zoé, now that he had read the invitation.

"I came to see if you could secure an invitation for me—and perhaps one for Charles as well," Zoé said. "And you should visit Sophie, for she is naturally unnerved by the thought of dining with the queen. She will need your support."

Thérèse was tired of being ignored. "Basile, tell me at once. Who is this Sophie? Do I know her? Why is the queen holding your engagement dinner?"

Basile rested the open letter on his knee. "Sophie

Twisden is English, and she is visiting Paris. The queen is undoubtedly looking for a way to enliven Versailles that will not cause her censure for stepping out of strict mourning. She wishes to host a private party that will unite the English in Paris—along with their ambassador, whom she well likes—and will include some of the French nobles. And what better occasion than to celebrate the betrothal of a marquis who was not thought to marry for years? It has the hallmark of success."

"What is this Sophie like?" Thérèse persisted.

Basile shot Zoé a look, which she had no trouble interpreting as she lowered her guilty eyes into her cup. She knew how little he appreciated that she had brought up the engagement at all.

"She is...*belle, talentueuse, charmante.* She speaks French with great fluency. You will surely like her," he said at last. He might be pretending about the engagement, but he had no need to pretend about her charms. They were in abundance.

"Do you think you can secure an invitation for me?" Zoé asked again.

He would like to have punished her for coming to stir up trouble, but the truth was, her presence *would* comfort Sophie.

"I will do my best." He narrowed his eyes on her. "But failing that, why do you not ask the Comte de Vaudreuil? I saw the two of you quite cozy at the Delbosc's supper."

Zoé colored, and her face took on a somber tone he was unused to seeing in her. "I do not wish to further my acquaintance with him. I depend on you to secure me an invitation."

Basile did not pry. It likely had something to do with Charles. He had not missed the way the Englishman had left the evening of the opera, his face like a thundercloud after watching Zoé flirt shamelessly with the earl. Perhaps Zoé was finally understanding what sort of a man he was. It occurred to Basile in a belated way that Sophie never flirted with anyone but him, not that he had seen.

"I will ask the Duc d'Orléans, and see if he might procure one," Basile said.

When Zoé took her leave, Thérèse eyed him with speculation. "So you have found a wife at last. It took you long enough after Claudia." After a moment, she added simply, "I am glad."

This was the moment to say something that would sow seeds of doubt that the engagement was not on such solid footing as everyone might believe, but he did not have the heart for it. The thought of ending the engagement was no longer a matter of course. In fact, if they were not already engaged, he quite thought he might like to court Sophie. And since he was not ready to be married, the idea was not worth dwelling on.

At last, Thérèse went to rest from the journey. Basile spent a short time with Achille, discussing the agricultural practices he was implementing, which at any other time would have interested him. Before his brother-in-law could be carried away by the topic, Basile had to plead a prior engagement so he could escape. And a short while later, he was knocking on Sophie's door. There, it was no surprise that he found her in the garden, her grandmother also having chosen to rest in the heat of the afternoon.

Sophie looked up when he strode out to her, then stood. Her gown was one of her more cheerful ones with broad stripes of cherry red and pink. It would have been impossible to walk out in it just now when the mood of Paris was somber, but he had to own how well she looked in it. Her expression, however, was wan.

He bowed over her hand, stopping short of kissing it but did not immediately let go. The idea of courtship had intruded once again in his thoughts. Despite himself, his heart beat a faster rhythm when he found himself near her. Perhaps he should suggest the idea of making their betrothal real.

"Did Zoé come to see you?" she asked.

He nodded. "And informed my sister of our engagement." He smiled at her ruefully, but she did not return it.

"What shall we do?" she asked simply. "It has all become so complicated. First my grandmother asking to live with you, then your sister learning of it. And now the queen is bringing our match into the highest public sphere with a dinner. It seems to me a dilemma entangled beyond remedy."

Basile stared at her, his heart heavy with her unhappiness. She did not deserve to be burdened with such worries, and it was fully his fault. "Won't you sit beside me?" he asked, giving her hand a light tug toward the stone bench.

She sat in a rustle of silk, and he sat beside her, careful not to sit as closely as before for fear it might result in the very thing that happened at the opera. His gaze fell to her dimpled chin, her elegant nose, her large brown eyes, and he absorbed all the details of her profile until she turned his way. He still had not answered her question. How was he going to get them safely through the court and society intrigue? Perhaps there was a simpler way. What once had been unthinkable, now seemed...not quite so.

"I promised I would see you through this." He shut his eyes for a moment as he gathered his courage. "I have asked once before, but I will ask again. Are you sure you do not wish to become betrothed in earnest? I never meant to compromise you by my prank."

"No!" she said, too suddenly as she turned her face forward.

His heart stuttered to a halt. He had almost thought she might wish for it. Without entirely being certain of his own feelings, he had begun to wish...oh, he did not know precisely what he wished for. It was too monumental to think it was marriage at this precise point in life. But he wished he could somehow continue to have Sophie Twisden in his life in some capacity. He wished she had not rejected him so summarily. That she did was more than a blow to his pride. It was a disappointment.

"No," she said again more calmly. "I have no wish for a betrothal that was established either to serve a pecuniary service or a convenient one. I merely wish to be guided by you on how to get through this dinner and its after-effects without enduring censure."

The fire he had felt the night of the opera fizzled. In its place was a sort of cold disappointment. He swallowed and brought his stare to the fountain in the corner of the garden whose bubbling sound filled the silence that had fallen. It was not until she had rejected his sincere offer that something like hurt pierced his chest. And yet, he would have to honor her by doing what she asked. He took in a silent breath, then let it out.

"We continue the charade until the end and convince the queen. We show all of society how deep are our feelings for one another, and then we shall have our fight and subsequent break-up. It will be out of sight of the public eye, for we do not want a scandal. But we will be sure that the reason that spreads is one of our choosing."

He turned to her, so she could see his determination.

"And as I promised, I will see you safely back to England. You have nothing to fear."

"You are most gallant," she replied, her voice revealing none of the playfulness he had come to know in her.

He could understand why. He had been anything but gallant in forcing this sham betrothal on her, and she was the one to suffer for it.

CHAPTER 18

"You sent word for us?" Grégoire inquired, entering the study with Armand on his heels. The *majordome* discreetly closed the door behind them. He had already provided the beverages in anticipation of their arrival.

Basile had been staring through the window, his hands clasped behind his back, and he now turned. The dinner with the queen was the next night, and he was still no further to knowing how he was to extricate Sophie and himself from this affair with their reputations intact. It had seemed once such an easy thing, but if his leaden heart was any indication he had grossly underestimated the task. "Have a seat."

They did so, and after pouring them some Burgundy, he asked, "Did you both receive your invitations?"

The queen had graciously allowed him to include the presence of three or four guests, and he had asked for Grégoire, Armand, and Zoé, along with her mother. He had learned from the ambassador, Lord Stormont, that most of the notables from the English society in Paris would be present. It would include Charles Arlington, whose presence Zoé hoped for. It would also include Cholmsley. At least Claudia would not be there.

"*Oui*," Grégoire replied. "Yesterday morning."

Armand also answered in the affirmative, adding, "And Vivienne will be there as well. I will present you, and I hope you will come to adore her as I do."

"And begin frequenting the jewelry shops on her behalf?" Basile could not help but tease.

"That privilege is mine alone, *messieurs*," was Armand's dignified answer.

Basile gave a smile which quickly fell. "Good. I shall need your assistance. This affair has blown out of proportion to a degree I did not expect."

Grégoire took a sip of his wine, studying Basile. "You have always been able to manage diplomacy, intrigues, and all their complications. What has changed this time around?"

Basile set his palm on the silk padding of the armrest and slid it forward to grab hold of the solid wood at the end. He pressed his lips shut, finding it difficult to come to the point.

"I think," he said, then paused as he swallowed over a dry throat. He tried again. "I think I fear for Sophie's reputation. In the past, I only had to worry about my own."

"You care for her," Grégoire observed.

"Why do you not marry her in earnest if you worry for her reputation?" Armand asked, a hint of reproach in his voice.

"I asked her. In earnest. She refused me." Basile's voice broke softly on the last sentence.

Grégoire leaned back in his chair and lifted his eyes to the decorative scrolls on the window frame above the curtains and let his gaze rest there, as though Basile's emotions were too private to witness. Armand had no such qualms.

"Did you tell her you loved her, and that you cannot live without her?"

"*Doucement*," Grégoire admonished with a lifted hand. "How do you know he does?"

"Any idiot can see it," Armand retorted. "He's been smitten with her from the first moment he laid eyes on her. Only, instead of wooing her in the proper fashion like any reasonable gentleman, he must go about with pranks and complications and dinners with the queen. Just tell her you love her."

Grégoire brought his eyes to Basile, who suddenly found it all too much. It was true. He did love her and wanted desperately not to have to live without her. If only she would believe it instead of assuming he was proposing out of courtesy. But perhaps he could convince her. Perhaps he needn't let her go.

Without thinking, Basile spoke the question that was foremost in his mind. "How does one go about convincing a lady of such a thing if she is determined not to believe it?"

Grégoire had a ready answer. "You must kiss her, of course."

Basile shot him a look as he delivered a wry retort. "It did not work."

"Ah."

Armand leapt to his feet. "Give her jewelry!" The suddenness and banality of his answer made Grégoire laugh, and even Basile offered a smile. But Armand was not to be put off. "No. Give her the jewelry belonging to the marquisate. Did your mother not have a set? In rubies, I think. And the set is well known. You will, at once, silence

La Bordenave and any whispers to the contrary of the engagement not being a true one. And you will convince your lady that you are serious."

Basile brought his eyes to Armand. That might actually work. "I believe you are right."

Grégoire set his glass down. "You will need an elegant gift for the queen, as well. A sapphire bracelet or some such thing. But she will find it natural for you to give the family set to your betrothed since this inheritance is passed down to each marchioness. You might even have the set cleaned when you go to choose the queen's gift."

"Excellent," Basile replied, his heart lifting. A smile returned to his face. That was exactly what he would do. "It is a great shame Claudia will not be present at the dinner to see me gift it to Sophie. That would silence her. She once admired the necklace when my mother wore it and was naturally not pleased when she learned my brother would inherit it instead of me."

"Oh, La Bordenave will see it," Armand said. "She will be there." Both Basile and Grégoire turned to look at him. "Vivienne told me. The widow has been making up to the queen, assuring her that she had no true allegiance to Madame Du Barry but has every allegiance to Marie-Antoinette."

"That woman," Grégoire said in disgust.

"Well, with so many witnesses, all of Paris will know my betrothal is real," Basile said. "I will now only need to convince my bride of it."

"Kiss her," Grégoire said again.

"He's done that," Armand replied.

Greg shrugged. "It never hurts to do it again."

After showing Basile to the door, Sophie had to sit with her grandmother who had heard him leave. It had taxed all Sophie's creativity to fabricate an equal level of joy when all she wanted to do was cry. It had been nothing short of torture when he'd asked her again whether she wanted to marry him in truth. It was unfair of him to take advantage of her weakness in that way. It was becoming more and more difficult to say no when she thought about the censure she was likely to endure, and the financial difficulty she must undergo, especially in trying to reimburse the sums Basile had expended on her behalf. It was especially difficult when he looked at her in that way, as though his feelings were in earnest.

The temptation had been very real, and Basile would have been well-served had she accepted him. That thought came in a moment of pique, but after brushing a tear away, she had to face reality. It was time to focus on enduring the dinner, the break-up, and the journey home to England unattached and somehow more impoverished than when she'd come. What was more, she now knew what it was like to receive the kiss of a man she not only found attractive, but with whom she discovered a likeness of mind—a humor of common cause. It was improbable she would find anything remotely like it upon returning home and burying herself in a life of simplicity and service.

Basile had promised to have his sister's maid come to assist Sophie and her grandmother with their *toilette* so they might be fit to meet the queen. The next day, the maid arrived with time to spare and assisted Sophie to dress in the double paniers that added more volume to the sides of her underskirt than she was accustomed to. The underskirt itself was a light gray silk with a Chinese pattern embroidered in black. Over this was a full skirt in a dark, charcoal gray with draws and ruffles as decoration. The bodice of the gown was cut in a square, trimmed with white ribbon—lower, too, than what she was accustomed to, but her grandmother assured her it was perfectly *à la mode*. She wore an accessory of a white silk flower around her neck, attached with dark gray ribbon. Her arms were bare of ornament.

Basile had shown remarkable kindness in having a pair of shoes sent along with the maid that contained a buckle decorated with paste, but which caught the candlelight when she put her foot out. When she wondered at how he had known her size, Mary admitted to having traced the outline of one of Sophie's shoes and given it to him. The shoes were black, with the heels and soles painted red.

With Sophie now dressed, the maid had her sit so she could set a cape around her gown to protect it and powder her hair white. The powder came from the marquis's household and had the usual cloves and other spices, but this time with a hint of bergamot, which Sophie adored. Whenever she could, she perfumed herself with the happy scent of oranges, because it inexplicably made everything seem hopeful. Now her fragrance would be orange spice.

The maid pulled her hair over a cushion set on the top of her head and pinned it in place before working on the *boucles* near Sophie's cheeks—trim rows of curls, the top of which was pinned back with a jeweled comb. As Jeannot had done, a large curl lay over her shoulder in a beguiling way to complete the *toilette*. Sophie stared at herself in the glass as the maid powdered her face and artfully applied color to her cheeks, her lips, and even to her eyes.

Sophie had grown more fashionable since arriving in Paris, but tonight it seemed the maid had worked wonders, for she hardly recognized herself as the English maiden who had stepped on to the French dock a few weeks earlier.

A knock sounded on the front door, which set Sophie's heart beating. *He is here!* Tonight was the big performance. Perhaps the last performance. Without Sheldon's continued support there seemed little reason to stay in Paris any longer. She would have to break the news to her grandmother, but she could never tell her of their deception. It would only break her grandmother's heart. Sophie knew the only heart that deserved to be broken was her own.

Then there was a faint knock on her bedroom door and Mary entered. "Your grandmother sent me to tell you she is ready to set out, and that the marquis is here."

"You may tell them both I shall be there in a minute." She smiled at Thérèse's maid, thanking her warmly, then sent everyone out of the room.

Seated, she stared at herself for another brief moment, then stood though she only had the view of her shoulders and below. She lifted her skirts and turned one way and another, admiring her figure, trimmed by the whalebone corset that pulled her shoulders back. It was an enchanting look. She would have purchased another corset like it if only she could find the means.

Sophie dropped her skirts, then, as reality crashed in. What good would it do to have beautifully fashioned corsets if she was going to become a paid servant? Or later, when she intended to hide herself away in some rural lifestyle, where she would likely end up raising chickens and turning the soil with her own two hands. It was a little terrifying, really, and she wondered if she truly had the courage to go through with it. It was one thing to say she would not marry without love, or at least a deep respect for her betrothed. It was quite another thing to envision the alternative—to live in the house she owned, but with an income so small as to reduce her to near poverty. She would have enough to eat and for a maid-of-all-work, but not enough to buy new clothes.

Her next thought was that to have known Basile, only to have to bid him *adieu*, sent such a lump to her throat and threatened imminent tears, she had to pull herself together by force.

She rubbed her damp palms on the towel near her nightstand, then grabbed a white, chicken-skin fan and fanned herself vigorously before stepping out into the corridor. She must get through this evening.

The marquis was making conversation with her grandmother, who wore the lovely gray silk gown that was in her possession since they'd set out from England. Basile ceased speaking at her entrance, and when he turned to look at her, he froze, his face a mask impossible to read. She wondered what was wrong. Had her hair been arranged too high on her head? Perhaps the rouge had been applied with too liberal a hand.

He moved forward then, holding her eyes in a way that tempted her to believe he truly appreciated what he saw—as if their engagement were real. She resisted that temptation.

He bowed and brought her hand to his lips, then kept it in his possession as he said, "You are enchanting, but I had expected as much. The queen will feel she has chosen to place her attention in the right quarters."

"You look very well, my dear," her grandmother added.

Mrs. Twisden's voice was stronger. She had assured

Sophie she was well enough to endure the evening, no matter how late it lasted, and indeed she looked much better than she had lately. Sophie could only hope that the queen would allow her grandmother to sit and rest when they arrived.

It was late afternoon when they set out from Paris for the ride to Versailles. It would take just under two hours if there was nothing on the road to hinder them. Conversation was light as they rode, the marquis on the backward facing seat, and Sophie frequently felt his eyes on her. She wondered if he was as nervous as she was. Likely not, since he had none of the complicated feelings she had that must force her to pretend to the queen it was the marquis she loved—only to then turn to the marquis and pretend she did not.

"Did you manage to gain an invitation for Zoé and Charles?" Sophie asked when they had ridden about halfway. Her mind had been taken up with so many things, she had nearly forgotten about that.

"Yes, for Zoé and her mother. You know Madame Sainte-Croix, do you not?" he asked, turning to her grandmother. When she replied she did not, he promised to introduce them before continuing. "Charles has already been invited along with much of the English crowd, and presumably Mr. Cholmsley." He made a wry face as he said it. "The queen allowed me to invite some of my own guests, so I also had invitations sent to Grégoire St. Pierre and Armand de Galladier."

Sophie nodded, then lapsed back into silence. Basile had not instructed her on what they were to do. As they approached Versailles, it felt to her as though they were racing to their doom.

The carriage slowed in front of the Petit Trianon, and

she recognized many of the English guests pouring out of other carriages. They all turned to her and curtsied or bowed, showing their recognition of her as the guest of honor. Before she had time to recover her serenity from such unwanted attention, Basile was at her elbow. His friend Grégoire rushed over to take her grandmother's arm.

And then they were inside on the black and white marble-checked floors of the entrance. The space was otherwise bare except for a couple of marble statues. They then walked up the broad marble staircase to the first floor where Basile led her past the guests in the antechamber and directly to the queen. He extended his leg and bowed deeply. "Allow me, Your Majesty, to present my fiancée, Mademoiselle Sophie Twisden."

Sophie curtsied very low. "*C'est un honneur, Votre Majesté.*"

The queen touched Sophie's arm and she rose. The fact of holding her breath made her lightheaded, as did fearing she might do something wrong or fearing the queen would find them out and be enraged.

But the queen smiled. "You are very lovely," she said in German-accented English. She then turned to the Comte de Vaudreuil who was standing at her side, ready to call over another guest. The queen's attention was withdrawn, and Sophie let out a quiet breath.

Basile pulled her close and whispered in her ear. "You see? You have worried for nothing. It was as simple as that."

Sophie turned to retort that they still had the dinner to get through, but the words died on her lips when she saw the expression on his face. The way he looked at her was filled with tenderness. The humor was there, but there was also another emotion she couldn't fully place. It was a duplicitous look, this—as though what he felt for her was real. She let out her tension with a soft laugh. "True."

"That was not what you were going to say, was it?" he asked.

She shook her head. "It is nothing."

Basile studied her for a moment, then said, "Allow me to leave your side. I wish to see your grandmother seated in one of the chairs near the window." He slipped her hand from his arm and took it in his own, squeezing it before letting it go.

Sophie smiled at him tremulously, trying to keep her composure, despite his convincing act. "Oh, yes. Please do. I worry for her health."

As he walked off, she was given a chance to admire his form. His handsome head of hair that was pulled back in a jeweled buckle, his strong set of shoulders that filled out his coat so beautifully. She allowed her gaze to follow his path and therefore missed Sheldon's approach. And at once, he was standing too close, towering over her, and bathing her with his hot breath as he forced himself upon her.

"Sophie, you have carried this farce all too far. You will not be able to recover from it."

She stepped back sharply and drew air. "When will you cease to harangue me? Why are you not yet convinced our betrothal is real?" Even as she said it, she could scarcely believe she could continue in such a boldfaced manner.

"Mrs. Betteridge is here. Did you think she would not be? She cannot fathom how you came to tell such a story, for she is sure never to have met the man. If this is one of your games, you had better put a stop to it now and come home. My name can still protect you, but we will have to leave France at once."

"I am astonished at your insistence," Sophie said quietly, "when I have made my feelings for you quite clear."

He moved forward again, but the soft, implacable voice of Lord Stormont came from her right. "Mr. Cholmsley. A word, if you please?"

Sophie exhaled quietly, grateful for the ambassador's delicacy. Unfortunately, the gift of his absence meant the curse of Madame Bordenave, who seized the opportunity of having no one to occupy Sophie's attention.

"Mademoiselle Twisden. What a happy night for you this must be." The widow managed to make the social nicety sound like it was studded with barbs.

Sophie exhaled and turned to face her. She might be out of her element and miserable, but she had one thing of her own that the widow could not take from her. *Her* character didn't change like shifting shadows. She could not only live peacefully with others, she could live with herself.

"A very happy night, as you see," she replied, a polite smile fixed on her face. "For we are finally able to celebrate our engagement dinner with my grandmother in attendance." She went to leave.

"However, one cannot but observe how odd it is that, though you are to be marchioness, you are still dressed so simply," the widow stated, her words carrying above the din. "The marquis is known to be wealthy. Where are the jewels your betrothed ought to be giving you? Where are the gifts that come from a man deeply in love?"

Sophie turned back. "I do not value Monsieur Gervain for his title or for his gifts. Therefore, I have not asked myself those questions."

"Perhaps you should." When Sophie did not reply, Madame Bordenave added, "Enjoy your dinner. Hopefully, you are able to get through it untouched by scandal." It was quiet enough that no one else heard, but loud enough for her words to hit her mark.

Despite her attempt at courage, Sophie was growing weary. She had few ambitions left, but getting through her dinner with the queen, without scandal, and without revealing the true state of her heart was pressingly one of them.

CHAPTER 19

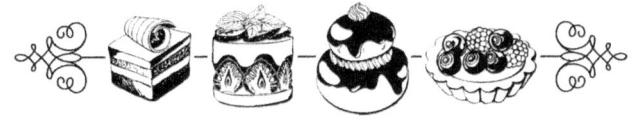

After Basile settled Sophie's grandmother into a comfortable chair in the antechamber, he turned to see Claudia speaking to Sophie, undoubtedly sending arrows her way. It was time to put a stop to this. He took a step toward her but was spared from performing a rescue. Armand brought a woman to meet Sophie who, from his beaming look, must have been his fiancée. One of the queen's attendants—Vivienne, if Basile remembered correctly. She was not much above plain, but had a sweet smile, and Armand was staring at her as though besotted. Basile watched Sophie relax under such kindness.

The servants had put out a simple buffet with *amuse-bouches,* but none of the guests seemed interested and continued to circulate the floor. Meanwhile, Lord Stormont, the English ambassador, went to pay his respects to the queen with Charles at his side. They held a short conference before they were released, and Basile followed Charles's progress as he moved to greet Zoé, who had just arrived with her mother. Basile gauged the potential court intrigue and tried to decide where he would best fit in.

After greeting Madame Sainte-Croix, the ambassador brought her to the circle of armchairs near the window, where she took a place near Mrs. Twisden. The windows were open, and a fresh evening breeze poured in. If only the evening was not fraught with potential disaster, it would have been a delightful gathering.

Zoé put her hand through Charles's arm and pulled him in Basile's direction, so she could give him a kiss on each cheek. "*Félicitations*, my dear friend," she said. Charles leaned over to shake his hand.

Basile raised an eyebrow at her. Zoé knew nothing of his intention to propose to Sophie in earnest. But he could not question her about it in front of Charles. So why the sudden show?

"I hope your sister was not too disappointed to be left at home," he said instead.

"She pouted." Zoé laughed. "Which was entirely understandable. She considers herself your friend, too. And she would have loved to have met the queen."

Basile smiled. "Tell her it is only a delay."

He lifted his eyes and caught Grégoire's regard near the entrance from the stairwell. Greg cast his eyes over to the end of the room where Cholmsley and Claudia were in deep discussion with the Comte de Vaudreuil. The latter raised an eyebrow and glanced over to the queen. Basile's heart began to beat queerly. He had been searching for an opportunity to control the tide of gossip, but it had been too quick for him.

Turning to Zoé and Charles, he said, "I may have need of you. Will you accompany me to fetch Sophie?"

"Of course," Charles said. Zoé wrinkled her brow in concern and turned to follow him.

Sophie was in high looks. Her cheeks were a delicate

pink that he thought had nothing to do with rouge. Powdered, clothed, and shod as she was so fashionably, she would be considered a classic beauty by anyone's standards. But it was her unadorned nature that shone the brightest to Basile and made him love her. She turned a smiling visage his way, pausing her words in expectation.

"Come, Sophie," he said. He held out his arm. His eyes were still on the queen, who was attentive to the French earl whispering in her ear. Sophie glanced at him with a worried expression but took his arm.

"What is it?" Armand asked, and Zoé leaned in to whisper to him as Grégoire moved to join them.

Basile led Sophie toward the queen, trusting his friends to follow. This was the most difficult moment, but he was poised for the battle and encouraged that every one of his friends would be at his side.

After giving Basile a sharp look, the queen disappeared through the large dining room, and the Comte de Vaudreuil came to meet him.

"Her Majesty wishes to speak to you," he said. "Now."

Basile acknowledged this with a nod. He could not resist adding, "I am not surprised, given all the whispers. I would only caution you to take care from whom you have the information that you carry to the queen."

Without waiting for a reply, he brought Sophie into the *salon de compagnie* where the queen had gone. She sat on one of the pink upholstered chairs there, waiting. Several of her attendants and courtiers flocked around her.

"Madame," he said, bowing again deeply. "You wished to have a word with me?

Her smiling demeanor was gone, and she looked down at Sophie's feet. "It is true then," she said to her. "You are wearing shoes with red heels when such a fashion is reserved for nobility."

Sophie's eyes widened, and Basile knew she had not understood the significance of the shoes he had sent her. Diamond-buckled shoes with a heel stained red, a sign of the *noblesse*. She had not known it was a sign that he intended to make her his marchioness in earnest. His intention was to propose to her with the rubies.

He hid all signs of agitation when he replied. "It is only natural, my queen, for we are to be married. She will therefore be a marchioness. If we have precipitated the wedding by her wearing the noble shoes, it was only for this dinner to honor Your Majesty." Sophie darted a worried look at him.

"That is all very well," the queen said, "but some of my attendants have said that you do not mean to marry her at all. That it was all done as a whim to humiliate your new queen by provoking me to take up your cause and look the fool. What have you to say to that?"

Spears of alarm pierced Basile. He had not counted on an open confrontation. Now it was imperative he convince Sophie their engagement was every bit as real as if they'd met over the course of a period of months, had walked together, danced together, shared intimate conversation, and had fallen head over heels in love. In fact, it was so. All of it was true. Except it occurred in weeks, not months.

SOPHIE WAS WADING THROUGH A NIGHTMARE. Could the queen of France have authority over an Englishwoman to the degree that she might put her in prison? Would Basile be punished in some similar way? She looked at him and caught his look of disquiet at the accusations the queen brought against them.

"*Votre Majesté*," Basile said, "I fear you have been fed misleading information, but it is not coming from us."

He reached into the left pocket inside his coat and pulled out a small black velvet bag. Taking it in two hands, he bowed and presented it to her. "This is, perhaps, an opportune time to present you with a small gift I brought with hopes that it will please Your Majesty."

The queen took it from his hands, looking at him almost warily. She opened the pouch and pulled out a bracelet made of a single row of sapphires of considerable size. Her eyebrows rose, for she had a weakness for jewelry. She brought her regard up to Basile.

Sophie saw the stones winking and glittering in the candlelight of the room. Much though she might wish to forget the widow's words, she could not help but think of what she'd said. That Basile had not bestowed any fine jewelry upon her, and that therefore he did not love her.

It was true, of course. He did not love her. This betrothal was made up, so he would not be giving her any jewelry. But for once, she thought how nice it would be to be cherished in that way.

"Along with this gift for you," Basile continued, pulling his gaze from the queen to glance at her, "I hope you will be pleased with the gift I have brought for my intended. I planned to use the dinner to present it to her, but I believe Fate has directed us on a different course. For what better timing than to present it to her in a more intimate setting with you at the head?" He turned and caught Sophie's hand.

She did not understand what he was doing. Was this

part of his scheme? He had never shared his plan with her, and she certainly hoped he had one. Basile reached into his other inside pocket and brought out another velvet bag, this one much larger and more worn. He presented it to Sophie with a bow.

"*Mon amour*," he began, causing her to freeze. This public endearment would make it much harder to pull back from. *Heavens! Is he thinking this through?* "This is my family's set of jewels. It has always belonged to the *Marquisat* de Verdelle ever since the title was created. As we are to be married, I now wish to gift them to you."

Wordlessly, she took it from him and opened the bag. Her fingers trembled with everyone's eyes turned her way. Out of the velvet pouch, a sparkling ruby necklace with several connecting stones in shiny gold slipped into her hand. A ring fell onto the floor, causing Grégoire to dart forward to catch it. He handed it back to Sophie. Then the rest of the contents, a pair of earrings and a bracelet, slipped out as well. She placed them back on top of the bag to keep a more secure hold of it all, then looked at Basile warily.

He turned to the queen. "*Altesse*, are you satisfied with the authenticity of our engagement?"

One of the courtiers was whispering in the queen's ear, and Sophie caught him saying the words "*les bijoux sont connus, sa mère les portait...*" He was assuring her that these were indeed the jewels that belonged to the family, for even his mother had worn them. Basile could not be giving such a sentimental and priceless gift to her in truth, but it seemed so cruel and unnecessary to take their charade to such a level.

"I am satisfied," Marie-Antoinette said. She directed a hard stare at Madame Bordenave, who stood at the back of the room watching the proceedings. "It looks as though your information was *une erreur*—unless you wished to make a fool of your queen."

Madame Bordenave had gone white, and she slipped out of the room, bumping into Sheldon on her way out. Catching a glimpse of the queen, not even he dared to make a scene. He, too, quickly disappeared from sight.

The queen smiled upon Basile. "Perhaps you might bring your fiancée to the *petite salle à manger* and help her to adorn herself with this charming addition, for I had noticed she was rather bare of adornment. Then we can move into the large dining room to begin the celebrations.

"*Je vous remercie de vos bonnes grâces*," Basile replied, taking the velvet bag from Sophie's hands, which had gone cold, and cupping the jewelry into one of his hands. Having thanked the queen, he slipped his other hand around her arm and led her to the small dining room the queen had indicated. She followed him numbly. The room was empty save for a servant, who quickly departed upon seeing them.

Basile set the jewelry on a table there, then said, "Turn for me."

Sophie was too stunned to think, so she obeyed him and felt the ribbon that held the silk flower loosen, then slide off her neck. It caused her to shiver, and she turned back around, lowering her voice to an urgent whisper.

"Basile, what are you doing? You cannot think to give these to me—or even to lend them to me. We have gone too far. We must tell the truth."

His blue eyes settled on her face, then he took one of her hands in his. "The truth? The truth, Sophie, is that I would like to hold this hand for the rest of my days."

He kept his brilliant gaze steady, which had the effect of hypnotizing her until he turned to the table to pick up the bracelet. He placed it around her arm, then fiddled with the clasp until he was able to shut it. Then he picked up the ring. "And I would like you to keep this ring, until I can choose one myself and place it there permanently."

Sophie's heart pounded with fear that what she thought she was hearing was part of the sham. Were there still people listening who needed to be persuaded? Surely, he could not have truly begun to love her.

He picked up the two earrings, gold wires that pierced the ears and allowed rubies to dangle from each. "*Hélas*," he said with a quick smile and a glance at her ears. "Yours are not pierced. These will have to wait."

He slid them back into the bag, which he returned to his pocket. Through all this, Sophie was helpless under his ministrations. She could not speak.

At last he picked up the necklace, which was intricate but not heavy, she found, when he took her by the shoulders and turned her gently so he could lay it across her neck. She felt the warmth of his hands and the cool metal against her skin. He brought her back around, then allowed his hands to brush the bare skin of her arms until he had her hands in possession of his own.

"*Je t'aime*," he said quietly. "I think I have from the moment I met you. Perhaps it was my heart that proposed publicly so we might be pledged until my reason could catch up. Please put me out of my anxiety and tell me you might come to love me back."

Sophie began to shake. She could not help herself, and neither could she smile. She was too fearful the attempt would cause her to burst into tears. "I am afraid..."

She stopped. It was too hard to get the words out around her constricted throat. Basile tightened his grip on her hands, his face growing dark with something like despair. And it was that look that forced her to speak.

"I am afraid I already do."

Basile's expression remained unchanged for a moment. Then his crystal-blue eyes went wide as a brilliant smile broke out on his face. "You already love me?"

She nodded.

"Ah, Sophie—"

And then she was swept up into his arms. He kissed her, and she responded by sliding her arms around his waist and clasping them behind him to hold him tight. And if the kiss at the opera had sizzled, this one burned, causing her stomach to swoop and her head to buzz, and her arms to want to pull him even closer.

Sounds of the servants entering pierced her fog, and Basile ended the kiss, pulling back from her. Cool air filled the space between them, and she blinked as though trying to clear the haze. When her eyes were able to focus, they filled with the vision of him watching her. He had her arms firmly in his grip and seemed to be attempting to absorb every inch of her face. At last, he released her.

"*Mon amour*, let us go celebrate our engagement dinner with friends, and even with foes. The friends will raise a toast and be happy for us *à l'excès*. The foes, I suppose, we shall have to put up with for one night, but we shall not care one whit what *they* do. After all, who invited them?"

EPILOGUE

30 décembre, 1774
Edinburgh, Scotland

Ma très chère Zoé,

It will come as no surprise to you that I nearly tore your letter in two when I broke the seal to read it. I've been so eager for your news, and your letter did not disappoint. I would have loved to have attended the masked ball in Versailles, but Basile says I must be presented to the queen first. Our informal engagement dinner did not count, of course.

But oh!—what news you had for me! It was not any ordinary ball it seems. So Mr. Arlington proposed to you at last! I am so very pleased. You asked what Basile would say when he heard the news, and he merely lifted his head from reading the newspaper to proclaim that it was about time.

You laugh, but perhaps you secretly agree with him. I am so delighted we shall be back in Paris in time to attend your wedding. I would promise to bring you some charming fabric or furbelow from our bridal tour if it weren't for the fact that the latest fashions are only to be found in Paris. But have no fear, *mon amie*—I shall indeed bring you something that will please you. Perhaps wedding dishes? Yes! It shall be a set of English china, of which I believe we need not be ashamed, though it is not a Sèvres.

I've been agog for news, and my patience was richly rewarded, for this day has brought me letters from both Thérèse and Vivienne de Galladier in addition to yours. Thérèse assures me my grandmother is going on very well, although of course you knew that. Thank you for inviting her to drink tea with you and for keeping her happily occupied in my absence. I can only be truly content knowing she is in good hands. And Thérèse promises that we will not recognize little Léonce for he is changed beyond recognition. I will have to take her word for it, but I cannot wait to go back and hug my delightful little nephew.

Vivienne positively assures me she is settling into married life as happily as I am. You will not tell her, of course, but this cannot be, for she is not married to Basile. However, I will own that Armand is as very gentlemanly a vicomte as they come, so of course she is allowed her modicum of happiness.

Ah, *mais oui!* How *could* I have forgotten? Speaking of being a gentleman, I was pleased to hear of Charles defending you in such a noble manner against the impertinent comte, thereby assuring you he is both madly in love with you and is possessed of a fiery passion that promises well for your marriage. You have much to look forward to. Much, *much* to look forward to.

No, I shall not tease you more on that head. In fact, I

will have to finish this letter at another moment, for Basile is attempting to tug the quill from my hand and will not be put off,

et donc...

La fin

ACKNOWLEDGMENTS

It has been immense fun working with Christina Dudley, Arlem Hawks, and Sofi Laporte on this series. We spent a year sharing historical research and relying on each other for our different strengths—including, but not limited to:

Christina's literary and historical knowledge (even the obscure), Arlem's specialty in 18th century France and period raiment, Sofi's knowledge of the Austrian princess turned queen and many other pertinent historical facts, and me for all things French, considering I've lived here for almost twenty years.

I still had to fact-check the French with my French translator, only to find I got plenty wrong. *Hélas*. It should all be fixed though, now.

Many thanks to Maxim, who—thanks to his studies of 17th and 18th century men's and women's clothing at the École du Louvre—has provided me with much insight that I was able to use in this book. Another huge thanks to Jess Heileman, my main author critique partner, for always bearing with me. Now it's my turn to focus on your book!

Thank you to Jo, who always helps me plot, and Theresa, who adds and removes commas, and generally saves me from embarrassment over things I should know, but don't. Credit goes to John Adams's wife, Abigail, who said something along the lines of it being better to go about *en nature* in Paris than to be unfashionable (a line I borrowed). Our tour guide mentioned it, but I couldn't find evidence of it. I'll take his word for it that she said it.

And thank you, to you, my readers. I'm grateful for you. Really and truly grateful.

The *Georgians in Paris* frolics began with *The Accidental Servants*!

He's marooned without a penny. She's in hiding to protect her virtue. As servants in the same Parisian household, can love be found between the schoolroom and the scullery?

Charles Ellsworth is a young Englishman on his triumphant Grand Tour when the dissolution of his family fortunes and his own recklessness leave him stranded and in debt. He enters service as a tutor in the household of M. Tremblay, with nothing but his wits and the kindness shown him by an elderly maid to depend on.

Pretty Jeanne Martineau played ingenue roles with a traveling theatre company before the manager absconded with the receipts. Now she works as a maid for the rakish M. Tremblay to avoid starvation, but escaping his groping hands requires she don the disguise of a hideous old woman.

When Charles glimpses Jeanne without her disguise, he quickly falls for the lovely young woman, but how can she reveal the truth without them losing everything to M. Tremblay's terrible ire and desire?

Books in the Georgians in Paris Series:

The Accidental Servants by Christina Dudley
A Match Gone Awry by Arlem Hawks
The Vicomte's Masquerade by Sofi Laporte
A Sham Betrothal by Jennie Goutet

ABOUT THE AUTHOR

Jennie Goutet is the best-selling author of twelve Regency romances, including the Clavering Chronicles, Memorable Proposals, and Daughters of the Gentry series. Her books have received first place in historical romance for the New England Reader's Choice Awards and have hit the number one spot in Regency Romance on Amazon. They have been featured on BookBub and Hoopla, and are translated into five languages.

Jennie is an American-born Anglophile who lives with her French husband and their three children in a small town outside of Paris. Her imagination resides in Regency England, where her proper Regency romances are set. You can learn more about Jennie's books and sign up for her newsletter on her author website: jenniegoutet.com or purchase her books at jenniegoutetbooks.com.

* Photo Credit : Caroline Aoustin

Printed in Great Britain
by Amazon